More Praise for *Orlando and other stories*

"Zelaya must have moonwalked out of the womb talking story. This debut collection of written stories is the invitation to break bread and gather in the most familiar and familial way, and to leave your formality with your tsinelas/chanclas at the door before you enter.

Zelaya's work draws us directly into conversation and place, whether it's looking over his shoulder as he answers the door to the three mysterious señoras standing in triangle formation, cooking with his abuelita, hanging out with his girl or walking toward his car to realize his windshield has been smashed (again). Whether the conversation is taking place in San Francisco's Mission District or on the hills overlooking Half Moon Bay, Zelaya's voice and storytelling style keep us rooted in movement with the characters and with curiosity for what will happen to them. These stories are hot, crispy lumpia right out of the fryer.

—Arlene Biala, Poet Laureate of Santa Clara County

"Let me introduce you to a unique voice, with sentences that shimmy to their own cadences, and dialogue that pops with the rhythm of the Mission District. These stories—and what stories!—engaging, moving, funny, and tragic and all at the same time.

Homeboy Norman is a gem—an honest story teller from the corazón.

—Alejandro Murguía, San Francisco Poet Laureate

To Jim,

thank you for the question
and conversation!

Norman A. Zelaya

9-8-18

Pochino Press
Oakland, CA

Library of Congress Control Number: 2017941774

ISBN: 978-0-9988758-1-1

Book design by Xiomara Castro

Printed in Berkeley, CA by Edition One Books

Para mi querida Claudia,
Te amo. Quiero estar contigo para siempre.

Acknowledgments: my mother, Dora Luz, my Abuelita Berta, my brothers and sister, Johan, Marvin and Lupita, my teacher Dr. Maryanne S. Berry, my collaborators, Darren De León and Paul Flores, and all my heads from San Francisco, too numerous to mention here but who influence me each day I step out onto the streets that I have walked all my life. You know who you is. Your voices are with me, encouraging with every step, *right on, homeboy, right on, little brother.*

Contents

All I Can Do Is Take Deep Breaths   6

Tommy on the Bus   48

Next Time   54

Would It Be So Bad If
Something Happened Between Us   58

Suspicious Man   101

Burn This Motherfucker
To The Ground   106

Orlando   118

All I Can Do Is Take Deep Breaths

I was careful not to make too much noise, the apartment was already a high-ceilinged vault and the smallest clink sounded through the air like a chant, so I stepped sure-footed like a deer, softly heel-to-toe as I moved around the kitchen mixing my energy drink, shaking my bottle with both hands to muffle the sloshing. There was no muffling the blender so I blended once LOUD for a minute and a half to make my protein shake and be done with it. It was 4:00 AM and the walls of our building were paper-thin. My neighbors would hear the sonic blast of my 12-speed blender and I'd hear their irritable groans as they turned communally to their other side tugging their blanket snugly over their heads. I wasn't being quiet for them. A general all-quiet hour had never been established (nor do I imagine would ever be adhered to faithfully, even half-ass heartedly) through an unspoken understanding between neighbors or a directive from the landlord or even a visit from the police for disturbing the peace. Upstairs, directly above us, there were all kinds of hammering and drilling and the dragging of excessively heavy shit for apartments as narrow and tight as ours at all hours, in particular after 9 PM. Two old *Nica* ladies lived in there, but I know it wasn't them doing home repairs. Sometimes, the younger septuagenarian knocked on my door for help. I'd answer the door to no one and then find her in the middle of the flight of stairs mired in fattened grocery bags, or worse yet, under the arm of the older septuagenarian, the two of them trapped mid-flight and needing two more flights to go. Other times, from the depths of the half dozen apartments above us, came a fuckin' caterwauling, a kind of professional off-key warbling unfit for any karaoke venue. I didn't mind the rumbling of the train under Mission Street. I didn't mind the wailing of fire trucks (although it had made me and other folks uneasy recently). I didn't mind the continuous banging of the gate and buzzing of my door to let folks into other apartments (it did bug me though how people didn't know their own fucking doorbell. I'd get *'ups, perdon. No sabia.'* And I'd be like, 'How the fuck you not gonna know?' Especially, when you been living here longer than me.) All that was living in the Mission for as long as I'd been here, which was all my life. But *this* – this disruption to LIFE, this vocal miscarriage fucking up everybody's favorite song always put me in a bad mood. *Who was that?* I never saw who it could be, but it sounded like a white woman from the conviction of her melodic bludgeoning. That was my guess. This woman dug the smell of her own shit. Then there were the romantic interludes of my neighbor, whose boudoir shared a common wall with my bedroom. So, in the wee hours of the weekend, on occasion a week night, came the slow, drawn out moans of a lover, mild complaints at first, hmm hmm whimpering even, but then building into a crescendo of maniacal screeching like no one had ever been boned in such a manner. It was some Groundhog's Day madness that moved you to *C'mon, no goddamn way.* Maybe it was for real, and the homegirl was dialed in to her sexuality, keen to her needs and threw herself into her orgasm as a liberated, empowered woman each and every time she fucked. And she found a dude with the skill and capacity and engineering required to ensure she made it to where she needed to go. I don't know, but it was damn loud and completely unsexy as an observer at 2:00 AM Thursday. My neighbor was a good dude though. Always greeted me, tipped his cap if he was on the phone. The one brother in the building who genuinely and formally welcomed me when I moved into my apartment. Any time I saw him at the corner bar, he always apologized and bought me my first beer. Always.

I was being quiet out of common courtesy but it wasn't for them. It was for Melly. I doubt I would have woken her though. She was sleeping the sleep of the dead, crushing the pillow and her hips hiked up like a giant baby, a tiny shine coming from the corner of her mouth. She was never going to know I was up so early and I'd be back from the gym and coming out of the shower by the time she woke. Even still, I tried to be quiet.

Recently, Melly was joining me for workouts, so much so that she bought her own membership and declared she was going to change her routine, set a goal and everything. When I touched her on the shoulder and shook her gently, she woke up with a feline stretch then bounded out of the bed with a ferocity and vigor and a slap on my ass, raring to go. But today was too damn early for her. I had an IEP meeting at 8 AM and I didn't want to break routine and miss my workout, so I sucked it up and just got up earlier. I let Melly sleep in. I left her coffee in the pot and her favorite vegan, cornmeal muffin from Arizmendi on the counter, gave her a kiss on her cheek, her springy black hair bunched against my face, and slipped out.

It was February and a COLD ass morning in San Francisco. Icy, nippy as hell. The two t-shirts and sweatshirt weren't enough and I walked quickly, almost picked up to a trot, to my car. I noticed the glowing frost that covered the parked cars, pearly white, sparkling in the moonlight. It was beautiful and the sky was clear, I could tell even in that early morning blackness that it was going to be a gorgeous winter day the moment the sun came up. The air would be clean, swept by hibernal winds, and the sky would be clear, everything visible from the Campanile in Berkeley to the

Mormon Temple in Oakland to Mount Diablo in Concord. I loved those days.

I was coming up on the block where I left my car. I hustled more, my key already in my hand. When my car was in sight, I filled with relief to get out of the cold, but that suddenly died in me. I was dulled, struck by a spirit-dampening reality. I wasn't concerned about the cold anymore. I slowed and pulled up next to the smashed out window of my car. The emptiness was exceptionally black compared to the dusty and frost-covered remaining windows.

Motherfuck me.

I opened the door and got in. I searched around the interior and nothing seemed to be touched or disturbed. My radio was in the glove box, my shades were in another compartment. None of my little papers were moved. Two cigars were in a pocket on the inside of the door. They only broke my window. And that hurt because it was the end of the month and payday, and now the little disposable income I had was going to repair a $200 glass pane. Fuck me... OK. I took a deep breath and decided there was nothing I could do about it at the moment. They broke my window. I'll get it fixed. Then a bitter chill came over me, not from the cold entering the broken window but from the realization that I left my work computer bag behind the driver's seat. I checked and sure enough it was gone. They broke my window, snatched the bag and were gone. It was my fault. The night before, Melly and I went to dinner. She had a doctor's appointment late in the afternoon and she wanted me, had asked if I could please go with her. She didn't want to go alone. It had been eighteen months since she discovered a lump under her breast, and she already had gone through two exams and consultations with oncologists and specialists (her doctors were taking good care of her, she said) and had been told it was benign, just some kind of mass of tissue and nothing to worry about, but they were going to monitor her for two years just to make sure nothing had changed. So, it was time for another check-up. I got off work a bit early to take her to the clinic. Everything was fine, there was no change. She was OK and they would see her in another six months. Melly was relieved and happy and we hugged and kissed and we were happy at seeing how relieved and happy we were together, so we went for sushi, our favorite. It was getting serious. It was exciting.

We ordered hot sake, miso with clams, and her favorite rolls. I had several kinds of nigiri. Sake. Tako. Unagi. Toro. Hamachi. Maguro. I loved the raw fish, the texture, the clean taste, the simplicity. We also ordered raw oysters, my favorite. We ate heartily, enjoyed every bite, enjoyed every moment of our company, laughed, talked into each other's ear, sometimes in whispers, other times for the chefs to hear at the bar. We made *brindis* and kissed and sat close to each other, knee inside knee. We ordered a second hot sake, *I* ordered a second hot sake, and we made more *brindis* – me to her health, to how happy we were, to sushi dinners once a week, to *hot sake*, to how pretty Melly was, to being a sexy bitch, then her to me, to a nice guy, to hanging out, to how kind and generous I was, *what, wait – I wasn't sexy,* yes, *yes,* to me being a sexy bitch, too, and to HOT SAKE and to us and romance and always remembering to go on dates and keep shit fresh. We fell into pleasant but animated conversation touching each other constantly on the shoulder, on the knee, a hand, letting one another know how much we liked the other. I drank the second sake; Melly had hot tea. We ended with a simple desert of green tea mochi and went home.

Melly drove us and found parking not too far away on a usual block in the neighborhood. We rushed home arm in arm and made love. Nothing like the spectacle of my neighbor's lovemaking, but vigorous, warm, a bit rough because Melly liked to move and turn and switch positions. It was athletic. We changed places, held moments, I listened to her, we squeezed each other, I motioned on her arm a few times to hold up, we waited and then climaxed together. I was in such a good mood, I had completely forgotten about my computer bag and hadn't a thought about it when I woke up in the morning.

Fuck. I stared out the windshield and thought about what I had to do – report it to my principal, report it to the IT department, fill out and file a police report. But at that moment, there was nothing I could do. Fuck it. I took a deep breath, started my car and went to the gym.

I went through my workout quickly and with a bit of extra energy. I got home and jumped in the shower. I thought about having left my bag in the car. Fuck. It was completely my fault. Too trusting thinking no one would trip about my cheap ass teacher car. Stupid, stupid, stupid mistake. I got out and dried, changed, and made something quick to eat. I went to the bedroom to get my classroom keys (luckily I didn't leave them in the bag) and my jacket and be out. I was on time.

Hey, lover.

Good morning, Melly.

How was the gym?

Fine.

What's wrong?

What do you mean?

Well, you're usually so full of pep. You tell me what you did, you tell me how you feel. You start doing some calisthenics like a hyped up Popeye. You're always in a good mood after a workout.

I exhaled slowly.

Someone fucking broke my window. AND stole my work computer.

Oh, no. I'm sorry.

Yeah, well, it was my fucking fault. I left it there. Completely forgot.

I'm sorry, babe.

Melly reached for and stroked my arm.

It makes me sad more than anything. I'm mad at myself, but I'm more sad that someone did this to me. Now I got to waste time and money to get the window fixed.

What a fucking drag.

Yeah, well…

Another deep breath.

It happens. I have to go. You gonna be here later? Your key is hanging by the door.

Thank you, and yes, I'll be here. I'll stop off after work and pick some things up for dinner. I'll make you something easy but nice, make you feel better.

I'll be good. See you soon.

I turned to leave.

Wait…c'mere you.

Melly hooked me by the waist of my jeans and pulled me back.

No, please. I can't. Plus, I still have this meeting to get to. I can't be late.

Alright. Then how about a big, steamy kiss goodbye.

Melly got up and hugged me, her arms clutched all the way around my shoulders. She leaned me to a side deliberately to kiss me, like in the old romance movies. She pressed her full lips against my thinner lips and inhaled long and raspy through her nose. I held onto her waist.

There. Now you're ready to go.

OK. Thank you. That was nice.

I want you to know that I really, truly like-like you, Tonio.

Oh. You like-like me.

Yes, I do, damn it. I can admit it.

That sounds serious.

It is serious. As a heart attack. I want you to remember that during your meeting. It'll help you.

Thank you.

Melly pecked my cheek and smacked me soundly on the ass. Then she dove back under the covers, rolling and twisting until she was pleasantly bundled up, smiling glad to be warm and cozy.

I tucked her in, turned out the light, and left her quietly once again.

Outside, the schoolyard was covered in shadow, a few older students trickling in through the big gate. I pushed the few large chairs I had around the round table and wiped it clean. I checked emails while I waited for the parent to show up. It was still early.

Hi, good morning.

Hey, you.

I printed a copy of the agenda, draft IEP and parental rights. And I've already added my new goals. All we'll need is to upload today's meeting notes and your goals and we're set.

You're very good, you.

Suzanne was our school's speech and language pathologist. She was also my partner. All my students were on her caseload and we worked very closely developing plans, coming up with strategies. I consulted her all the time. She kept our meeting schedule, reminded me of dates and to complete rating scales. Suzanne kept me organized. At work, she was my better half.

I'm going to need you this morning. I'm not at my best.

What's wrong?

Just dealing with some nonsense. I'm OK. Nothing to be worried about. Just a fucking nuisance I have to deal with. My fault really. I'm really distracted is all.

Well, Sylvia is taking notes. This meeting is just an annual. You'll give present levels, we'll go over current goals, make recommendations and get out of here. We'll be done in less than an hour.

Like I said, you're very good.

You just let me know if you want me to handle the meeting.

No. That's fine. I can manage the meeting. I want to.

We'll have to see if mom brings the babies. That always takes up time.

No. Mom said she found someone to watch them. We'll be good.

The shadow had retreated halfway across the yard, and now there were more children and the noise of chatter and play was clear through the large windows of my classroom. It was a beautiful sky blue day and the children were joyfully playing in the sun, bouncing and kicking balls, gathered at corners of the yard to share and shriek and laugh, sitting quietly on the benches waiting for the first bell and the school day to begin.

The meeting moved along with our assistant principal, Sylvia, taking notes and Suzanne handing me documents as I reviewed the agenda to the mother and tended to each bulleted item. We each did our part stopping to make sure mother understood and giving her the space to add her expertise. She mostly nodded and told us to continue. We reviewed services, educational placement (her son would continue with me) and asked her a last time if she had any questions, comments, concerns.

She smiled sheepishly.

Bueno, sí maestro. Yo tengo una duda.

¿Sí, que es su duda?

Maestro, what can I expect from my son? I hear you tell me that he is improving and you show me what he's doing in class, but when I talk to him, when I ask him something, he just repeats what I ask him. I don't know what he's thinking most of the time and he can't tell me what he's thinking. We don't have a simple conversation when we sit in the kitchen. I ask him about his day and he just tells me yes, I don't know, or he says nothing. Unless, it's about that game, I'm not sure what it's called – Minecraft. Then he doesn't stop.

We all laugh politely with her.

When we go to a party or a gathering, the people watch all the little things he does and then they ask me, 'What's wrong with your son?' and I don't know what to say. I feel sorry for myself. What do I say, *maestro*? I know you've told me what my son has. He's autistic. But can you please explain to me again what is wrong with my son?

Mother was young. I was now at the age where most of my parents were younger than me, or at least, around the same age. I looked into her eyes. She was still smiling, but only because she didn't want to fall apart and start crying. Her eyes were moist and there was a slight tremble in her full cheeks. She was a very young mother of three. I thought about my mother at that same age, already with all four of us, and it seemed to me an utter impossibility. How was mama ever that young with so many kids and alone? How did she carry on? Suddenly, I felt the eyes on me. Mother looked at me with her quivering smile, and Suzanne and Sylvia were looking at me, too, waiting for my response.

I smiled as kindly as I could, readjusted myself in my seat to sit a bit closer. I took a breath and began, finally.

First, there is nothing wrong with Mateo. Mateo is Mateo, and I think he's great. He's kind and cares about his classmates and he's funny. He likes to tease me most. Mateo is a person with autism, and he's learning that about himself. My job is to teach you how to understand Mateo's needs and what we can expect from a person like Mateo. Then it becomes your job to educate your family and the bigger community about someone like Mateo. First, you tell them, 'There is nothing wrong with Mateo. My son is autistic. This is how he deals with the world.' And I can help you with that if you need me. Mateo is great, *señora*.

It felt funny calling someone that much younger than me *señora*.

Gracias, maestro.

As latinos, how many horrible things happen in our culture and we say that's normal? How many times do we watch a man do something abusive, violent and no one says,

'What's wrong with him?'

Sí, es cierto, maestro.

Here is what we can expect from your son. Mateo is going to speak and use words to express what he needs and what he wants. We have to model and teach him that. It doesn't always occur to someone like Mateo to let someone know when he needs something. For example, when I see Mateo walking in circles in the classroom, I know he needs or wants something. I have to step in his path and ask him, and he does tell me.

Sí, maestro, I notice him do that at home.

OK, so these are the things we need to pay attention to when working with Mateo. Mateo is going to play with other children and work in groups. We know this is hard and a challenge for people like Mateo, but he can learn it. We have to show him.

Maestro, what is Mateo going to do when he grows up?

I don't know. My hope is that he will have choices. I hope all my students will have choices.

Yes, but will he be able to have a job?

He can. It will be a challenge and he'll need a lot of support, but all children need support to be independent in their lives.

Mother relaxed into a genuine smile, pleased to receive good news, glad to have hope.

The last minutes of the meeting was a back and forth of questions and answers regarding details about Mateo's goals and supports and strategies for mother to help him at home. Suzanne gathered signatures from the members of the team, demonstrating with her index finger where mother should sign. We rose together, shook hands and thanked each other for a productive meeting. We said goodbye and made our exits.

I'll upload the notes and signature page. Do you think you can have your goals done by next Wednesday?

I'll have them done before I leave for home today.

Thank you. You did a great job with mom.

Suzanne gave me a half squeeze then left.

The schoolyard was bathed completely in sunlight. It was full of children, and some parents huddled together in conversation sipping satisfied from white cups of coffee.

We had finished our meeting early. There was just enough time to get ready for the start of the day.

Afterschool, I made sure to add my new goals to that morning's IEP before leaving for the weekend. I reviewed the notes and added some details I thought important. I checked dates and checked appropriate boxes, dotted I's and crossed my T's before submitting the plan electronically to the district. I closed the windows and turned off the lights.

I grabbed my jacket and looked around once more before leaving.

It was cold outside. Luckily, I lived just around the corner. I walked home in five minutes.

I unlocked the door quietly. I didn't want Melly to hear me come in. I ducked into the bedroom to put my jacket away, but when I stepped out, Melly was already coming down the hallway with her hand extended for mine. She gave me a quick kiss.

How was your day?

Good. It was good, actually.

Melly led me through the hall to the living room and sat me down. She went to the kitchen and brought out two glasses of red wine. Sade was playing from a stereo on the counter.

Can I have a beer instead?

Have wine with me first. I bought some nice cheeses. Besides, I like the smell of wine on your breath.

Melly reached over to a wooden platter on the coffee table and fed me a small wedge of dull yellowish cheese.

Do you like it?

Mmm. Toasted, like burnt *cajeta*. Nice crystals. Firm but flaky. Robust, lots of flavor. That is aged Gouda.

Goat's milk Gouda. Do you like it?

Mmmmm. You're taking care of me. You know cow

milk does me wrong.

Try it with this.

Melly fed me a dried black fig.

Mmmhmm.

Right…right.

Mmmm.

You get it. Kinda sour, tart. Creamy and chewy. Yeah. All the tiny seeds bursting. You're digging it, right?

I drank my wine freely, closed my eyes to focus on the pleasure. Melly fed me another kind of cheese.

Hmm. Spicy, full-flavoured yet well balanced.

Would you say profound or complex?

Yes. Hmm… Smooth, firm.

Bold, rich.

That's Gouda, too.

No, it's a kind of gourmet Gouda. It's called Beemster.

MmmMmmmmm. You are taking care of me.

Melly half climbed onto me and kissed me, disregarding the glass in my hand. We had a bit more of the cheeses plus figs and some nuts and honey.

Dinner is ready.

She led me to the dining table, which was half in the living room and half in the kitchen. It had belonged to my mother. It was too big for the apartment but it was still very nice, and gave me more spots for people to sit when folks came over.

Melly grilled fillets of some kind of white fish with grilled asparagus and mashed potatoes. She offered me slices of a marbled bread.

This was easy for you to make?

Easy peasy lemon squeezy.

Thank you.

Do you still want that beer?

Oh hell yes, I need a beer.

Melly pulled out a large can of Japanese beer and split it between us. We raised our glasses and ate. I ate quickly, chewing vigorously. Melly took her sweet time, chewing each morsel for a measured and even numbered amount of time.

How was your meeting?

It went well. I was super distracted, but I managed to keep it together. I mean I have to. Parents are nervous and afraid. They don't know how to help their kids. It's scary, man. So, I better act like I know what I'm doing. I had help though. But it's tough. I'm holding space for all those students. Little goofballs.

I wonder what that's like – having a sexy teacher be my kid's teacher.

Is that what I am now – sexy?

Some looker you are.

I thought I was just a nice fella.

A real knockout.

I'm no dish like you though.

Sure you are, doll.

You're a real tomatuh.

You're no slouch yourself, handsome.

How 'bout another splash of that giggle water, Jane?

All we have left is this hooch, sailor.

That'll do.

Melly got up to serve me more wine. I continued our playful banter.

[*long whistle*] What a pair of gams!

What – these pins?

Easy on the eyes.

Made for digging the jive.

Cutting a rug.

If I found the right fella.

Hold on, sister, I don't know if I'm your beau.

I'm not talking sidecar, Jackson. Just some big palooka to hold me up while I swing a wing.

A main squeeze.

Something like that, lamb.

We giggle a bit, clink our glasses. Melly has big brown eyes. I loved how she looked at me, like she held me, super into me.

Are you keen on me?

I'm your fever.

I didn't know it was catching.

Oh, you caught a case alright, buster.

Feel my forehead.

Melly climbed onto the table and rested her forehead against mine.

You're burning up, Jackson.

Then I guess I got a fever.

You said it.

Melly brushed my plate aside. Carefully, she set my glass to a safe spot then grabbed me by the shirt, and pulled me in for a kiss. Her mouth hovered over mine, her lips touching down, sporadic like a tornado, before landing finally, drawing me in taking my breath, her grip tightening my collar around my neck. I just kept my eyes closed like a nervous but acquiescent teen.

Hipódromo means race track in Spanish, and language-wise it helps to understand how horses are related to hippos. My father taught me the word when I was a boy. I didn't understand why there was a statue of a jockey on a horse outside the entrance of Tanforan Mall in San Bruno, and he said *'aquí había un hipódromo'* a long time before I was born. It was for thoroughbreds. You know, like Seabiscuit, racing champions, powerful well-bred horses. They eat better than me and you, he joked. But not really funny. It was probably true. The track at the Polo Fields in Golden Gate Park was never for racing, just for folks to walk and exercise their horses, which was always a trip for me. How are you gonna have a horse in San Francisco? Hella money, blood, as my homeboy Eusebio put it. You buy what the fuck you want. Shee-it. A couple of cyclists in aerodynamic helmets circled the paved inner track as I walked along the outside edge of the horse track. They easily lapped me several times in ten minutes as I moved at my leisurely pace. I ran other times, but today I needed to walk. It was an overcast day and it was late in the afternoon, the shadows beginning to creep onto the grass of the infield, and the temperature beginning to drop noticeably. There were few other people around besides the two cyclists locked in informal competition. They pushed each other while us pedestrians paid each other no mind whatsoever. I came at this time of day precisely because there would be few, if any people around. The chill got to me and I picked up my pace. When I was in high school, I worked at the boathouse at Stow Lake, which was also in the park, renting rowboats and little motorized boats to the public. Actually, I got there early in the morning to scrub the duck shit off the dock and boats then helped people in and out of boats for the next seven hours. Summertime was busiest with all the tourists coming in and the weather being okay enough to be outside, sometimes it was even hot, but no matter the weather, summertime was a damn *hormiguero* of people crawling out of the woodwork all over the docks and boats. People are demanding when they're on vacation. The foreigners were nice enough though. They seemed to make an effort to have fun, like the time I had to retrieve three German women on a rowboat, way tipsy and past the time the boat was due back. They offered me some wine and flirted with me, but I was too young and they too cool and me with too much of a work ethic (and no game). No way I was going to risk my job just to listen to ladies tell me I'm cute. That shit was never going to work out, but it was fun. American tourists were so so. One time, a large man from Texas wearing a safari hat walked up to me while I was hoisting a motorboat out of the water. I saw him coming, so I stopped what I was doing and waited patiently for him to speak. He bent over to say something, then something else came over him, something dawned on him, and he asked me if I spoke English. I smiled at him. Yeah, man, I speak English, I said. How can I help you? They were alright. Just didn't know any better sometimes. But without a doubt, the worst pricks were residents from the neighborhood. Folks who lived right near the park talked to you like they were ordering hamburgers in a drive thru. Spoke at you requesting all manner of unreasonable shit. Yelled at you, Hey buddy!

like that was okay. Talked to you with their eyes in their pockets or wallets or purses, their eyes above you at the menu, or to their watches. One scruffy dude came to the lake with three little blonde girls and a baby in his arms. When I told him that all five of them could not go in a rowboat, he had a foaming at the mouth fit. It was nothing for him to yell at a 16 year-old boy in front of his girls, in public. He only mentioned three kids when he rented the boat, so it was cool in his eyes. I explained the insurance did not allow five people in a rowboat. He told me the baby didn't count. I explained if the baby fell in the water and drowned, it would count. He blew his raggedy dirty-blonde top and called me an asshole and all kinds of other words. Then he *demanded* to see my boss. I motioned to the ticket booth and he marched up with his paperdoll string of girls in tow, the baby's head bobbing violently as he huffed to the opening in the glass. I didn't hear what he said, but I saw my boss shake his head 'no' calmly and then the fucking rock n roll histrionics, pounding on the counter, stunned baby wide-eyed and flopping about, and the little girls asking 'What's the matter, daddy?' and again 'That asshole won't let us on the boat!' My boss and I smiled at one another as the dude dragged his kids out of the park. *Dick.*

It was cool though to work in the park. I liked the shady quiet of the morning and how the rush and din of 19th Avenue faded away as I stepped under the canopy of trees. I slowed and sometimes stopped altogether when I was inside the cathedral of redwoods, the light streaming down through the branches, the softness of the fallen needles, the smell of the morning wetness in the earth. Walking through that garden gave me peace, helped me leave whatever sadness I was carrying to work on the 22 Fillmore, so when I got to the boathouse, I usually had on a smile. I still loved to walk in the park for that reason. It made me smile.

Melly sent me an instant message.

what r u doing, sailor

Working on a lesson plan and answering emails at the same time.

good job, abercrombie

I try.

i'm wrapping up finishing touches for our benefit. be at office late then i'll swing by.

OK. You have your key.

tell me something sexy

Three students went home today with violent diarrhea.

yuck. really tho. tell me something sexy

You are the eel's hips.

bee's knees

I got a fever.

you said an earful, sweet patootie

I'll see you later, angel. You'll find me with nothing but a smile.

=)

When I got out of bed to get ready for the gym, Melly got up with me. First, she threw both arms around my waist and refused to let me go. She anchored us to the bed with her well-muscled lower body. I was able to drag her partially off the bed then she popped to her feet and we got ready. She made the protein shakes while I mixed the energy drinks.

It was cold, nearly so as it was earlier in the week. The sky was clear again and stars pinpricked the black ether.

Fuck! It's cold.

Melly hustled along and I jogged beside her. The car was just ahead on a corner. Then Melly saw it first.

Motherfucker!

I couldn't see well enough in the dark, and maybe I just didn't want to believe it, but when we got under the lights at the corner, it was undeniable.

Motherfucker!

The rear window was completely smashed out and everything that was in back – copy paper, magazines from the Giants championship, 2 lb hand weights, jumper cables, a seat cushion, the cover that came down over the trunk space when the hatchback was closed – was strewn all over the street. A jean jacket that I had been keeping back there because of the cold was missing.

Why? Motherfuckers just stole from me a week ago. God damn it!

Melly put a hand on my shoulder as I stared down at all my shit in the street. She stood close to me but I felt her giving me space at the same time. She didn't say anything to me. What could she say?

I opened the hatchback and shook out the glass with a gym towel. Melly began to pick up my things from the street.

No. Leave it.

You don't want your magazines?

No. It's fine. I don't want them to have any reason to come back.

But you love these magazines.

They're just old magazines.

Babe, they're collectibles. I know you want them.

I stood quietly with my hands on my hips, breathing deeply. I stared into the emptiness of the open hatchback.

OK. But fuck everything else. Leave it all in the street.

Melly gathered the magazines, brushed off the covers, and set them in a clean corner stacked neatly. She helped me sweep the rest of the glass out of the back and then we cleaned off the back seat, carefully picking bits of glass one at a time in the darkness not thinking about the cold anymore, only worried about cutting ourselves in the pre-dawn hour, but we didn't stop until it was free of any broken material as far as we could tell. We shook out the floor mats, replaced them and finally slid into the seats.

Thank you, Melly.

I'm sorry.

There's nothing for you to be sorry about.

I know, but…

You feel bad for me. I know. It'll be alright.

I turned the ignition and grabbed the gearshift. Melly put her hand on top of mine and we drove off like that holding hands, quiet, the radio turned low, only an occasional rush of static escaping from a bad speaker.

After the gym, Melly and I showered quickly and got changed. I was dropping her off downtown. She had some meeting at City Hall, early, and asked if I could do her the favor. Of course, I could. I sped her downtown after stopping for a cup of coffee. Civic Center wasn't too bad at that hour. It would soon be worse with all the narrow One Way streets and forever construction on downtown plots. I pulled up right in front of the City Hall steps. Melly leaned over for a peck and hopped out, click clacking up the sprawling dignified steps of the bureaucratic structure. I watched her sashay, step determined and confident. She turned back and gave me a tiny wave with her fingers. What's a dame like you doing with a Joe like me, I thought.

I was numb the whole day at work. I struggled to stay focused and walked in a daze through the routines asking my paraprofessional to tend to any student asking for a little extra attention. I couldn't do it. I couldn't hear the extra voices today. Couldn't 'yes' each call quickly enough to satisfy them. I wasn't as present as I usually was and the kids asked my para, *Maestra Adela, qué pasa con Maestro?* I managed the students through read alouds and the calendar and recess and library and English Language Development and interruptions from the phone, the office, the Department of Social Security, a parent with just a little question and an even tinier follow-up question, not wanting to take up too much of my time, a call from the nurse, a call from a colleague asking if I could help her with a student in the hallway, and literacy centers, and computer lab and group interaction and finally clean up and get ready for the buses. I asked and leaned on *Maestra* Adela as much as I could, and somehow got through the other requests for my time and help and opinion. I didn't give out homework when the students asked for it. Not today, I said. Don't worry. Tomorrow. But one kid's parents was going to ask for homework and it was part of his plan to earn time on the iPad at home, and another student piped up asking for homework because he wanted work, too, and soon others were asking for homework because monkey see monkey do, *what's wrong with you guys trippin about homework,* and so I sent *Maestra* Adela to make some quick copies, stuffed them into each backpack and sent them all home, bye-byeing repeatedly, waving, and acknowledging yes, *sí, sí,* Ricardo C., *sí,* I will see you tomorrow, *sí, mañana* Skywalker car, *sí* Ricardo, I'll be here tomorrow, *sí* we'll play tomorrow, *primero trabajar sí, después jugar.* Bye Ricardo, bye. They watched me, small hands pressed to the glass, and waved as the buses drove away.

Melly listened to the radio as we spoke. I could hear it playing quietly in the background. Sade. "Hang On To Your Love".

What station are you listening to?

It's not the radio. I'm playing a CD.

Oh. It's nice.

I love Sade. That is a bad ass lady. She always puts me in the mood.

In the mood for what?

For eeeeverything. *Rrrrr!*

We laughed easily.

What are you doing, puddin'?

Before you called, I was just laying here, in the middle of my bed, thinking. Hands on my belly, looking up at the ceiling, thinking. Digging the quiet.

I was still looking up at the ceiling, one hand on my

belly as I held the phone to my ear.

What are you thinking about?

The two broken windows. The cost. I think what am I going to do. Then I answer my own thoughts. I'm going to wait and pay for it. All I can do.

I'm sorry, Tonio. I wish I could help.

Nevermind. It'll be OK. Right now, I'm just listening to the music in the background, and thinking about how good it makes me feel. Soft. Calm.

We both listened quietly for a few moments.

I can't believe it happened twice in a week.

Yeah. Once is bad enough, but this feels personal. Like someone intends to fuck with me.

Do you think it could be?

I figure they got over big the first time, then recognized my car and thought I'd be stupid enough to leave more shit in my car. They checked just in case.

But do you ever think someone might be trying to do you wrong? Like, maybe an old student?

My students…naw, my students are too little.

Not your current students, you dork. I mean, maybe a former student all grown-up and still mad at *Maestro* Antonio for giving timeouts liberally?

Ha ha. Hmm…no. When I first started teaching, I was like the kids. I was emotional. I got easily triggered. I met

36

my students with the same energy and fire they had. I may not have made the best decisions, and I definitely could have handled situations a lot better. But I was young. I didn't have the skill yet. But I think my students knew I cared about them, I think they knew I wanted the best for them and I was fighting for them and not with them. I'm sure some of them got super angry at me. But in the end, we laughed a lot. We played. We had fun, if not actually learned something.

Sade played on, "Never As Good As The First Time".

I think about one student sometimes.

Mmhmm…

The first day he was in my class, he sucker punched a kid when they were all lining up to go home. The other kid was getting his backpack, and this student turned around and just punched him. He felt something moving behind him and that set him off. Over time, he got better, but not much. He'd come around for a few weeks and then fall back into his aggressive shit. He refused to do work. He stole things out of people's backpacks. He said mean, nasty things. He didn't fight much again because the other kids bowed up on his ass, and he wasn't quite as tough as that first day. He was more pest. A lot of hate in that kid. Pain. He had his good days, but he needed more than we could offer in that classroom.

You did your best.

I did, and I know I could do better now. Hindsight,

right?

20/20, palooka.

Whatever he was in my classroom, his mother struggled with him more at home. We had a meeting once, and she started to break down a bit. She told me she went to see a reverend who was touring in the community, and she waited in line to ask for *una sanación.*

What's that, a cleaning?

A healing. She asked the reverend to pray for her son and heal him. Like putting your palm to a cripple's head and that person popping out of the wheelchair, dancing a jig.

Cutting a rug.

Digging the jive.

What did you say to mom?

I told her it was good to stay positive. We had to continue to give her son opportunities to do well. We were not going to give up.

How old is he now?

He has to be around 16, 17 years old.

You think it could be him? He might resent you.

No, no. It wasn't personal. That dude didn't like anybody.

Melly sang a few verses. *In heaven's name / why are you walking away / hang on to your love/ in heaven's name / why do you play these games...*

What is your day like tomorrow?

Oh man, it's a big day! I have to get to the Green Room early and help set up for our fundraiser for *El Centro*. Put up streamers. Tie balloons. Put my personal touch on the centerpieces. The flowers are all me. It's going to be a big party, Tonio! Fun, fun, fun!

Sounds like it.

You bet your sweet patoot. I have you on the list. You're coming.

I think I can make it.

That wasn't a question. You are coming. Make sure you go home first and change. Don't wear what you wear to work.

Why not?

You're not coming to the dinner in paint and snot-covered khakis. You have to doll up, doll.

Ha ha. OK.

OK.

I'll let you go then. You have a big day tomorrow.

No, wait. Listen to this song with me. Then you can go.

Feels like / your mine / feels right / so fine / I'm yours / your mine / like paradise…

OK. Now you can go.

I hung up. I laid my phone to the side and rested both hands on my stomach. I shut my eyes and imagined the streamers and flowers and a small plate of cake. Melly fed me tiny pieces on a white plastic fork. She wiped frosting on my nose and laughed at how silly I looked before giving me a big kiss and fed me more cake. I laid still on the bed and smiled.

The sun was well up above Potrero Hill and shining rays down 23rd Street all the way to the hills of Noe Valley. I watched the long shadows of trees and telephone polls stretch along the sidewalk as I walked to my car. I took my time. I was headed to a workshop at the district office; not teaching class that day. So, I was in no rush. Two partners drinking from a brown bag walked along ahead of me. They were in no rush either. They stopped next to my car and posted up against the wall. One noticed the broken rear window, craned his neck to study the damage then turned back around when his partner asked for another sip.

I walked up and unlocked the hatchback. I shook out what little glass Melly and me had missed. I was about to pull the door down, but I stopped. I scanned the inside to see if anything else had been disturbed. I thought about everything that was taken from me. My laptop. CDs. Jean jacket. A cable to plug an iPod into the radio. It was a sad feeling and I found myself staring into space.

$450. $450 because it was the back window to the hatchback and I definitely did not have the money to repair it. Not this month, anyway. The insurance would reimburse $200 of it, but first, I had to come up with the total amount to get the work done. Then I could file for a check. That wasn't going to happen until March. So, I took another deep breath (those were free and fucking plentiful) and resigned myself to driving around with a broken hatchback window, a constant chill inside as I drove and the heater forever on, blowing warm air on my feet.

Finally, I snapped out of it and slammed the door shut. I was about to pull out when I noticed someone run up along the passenger side waving to get my attention.

Hey, homeboy, can I ask you a question?

Yeah.

What did they take that they had to do all this?

Nothing, man. Nothing worth anything.

He bowed his head in disappointment.

I'm sorry, brother. I'm sorry they did that to you. You take care now, homeboy.

Right on.

He raised his beer to me in *salud* and stepped safely away from the curb as I pulled out and zipped to Harrison, where I made a left to get to my workshop. I looked in the rearview mirror as I turned. The homeboy still held up his beer, raised high to make sure I could see it.

Melly and I sat back on the sofa our feet stretched out on the floor. We watched a movie and took nips from a cheap bottle of red wine. I adjusted the light from the lamp on the small end table.

You know, I've been thinking about you, lover.

It's nice to be thought of.

No, for real, I've been thinking about your predicament.

Yeah.

Yes, it's really messed up, and I know how much it's troubling you. I see you. It's eating you up.

I admit it distracts me. It's hard not to think about it when I'm driving and a fucking polar wind is hitting the back of my neck.

That's awful, right.

It fucking sucks vulgar objects.

Well, I can help you.

What do you mean?

I can give you the money.

I don't know, Melly.

What don't you know?

It's not your problem.

I'm spending enough time here. It's like I almost live here.

It's still not your responsibility.

We stayed quiet. Melly thought a minute.

We can make it a business transaction. I can pay you for services rendered.

What services?

She looked devilishly at the ceiling, like a big florescent bulb lighting above us.

Dick services. I can pay you for your dick. HA!

A big ha. Melly gave me a fiendish smile and leaned forward to kiss me with a loud smack.

It seems to me you can buy a whole lot better dick with $400 - $500.

Oh, I know! One that spins and twirls, runs one way then runs back and then back again *whir whir whir* unh unh… one with pearls, or one with a little dolphin that comes up to the happy place, and one that hums and purrs – or maybe that's just me *hee hee*. Oh shit! One with a remote control – oh my god, I love my vibrator!

It was a bit surprising to hear Melly admit out loud that she owned a vibrator, but Melly was a liberated woman of the world, hella cool like that, she loved to explore and loved and owned her orgasm. Of course, she had a vibrator. Likely, two.

But I want to help you, Tonio. Let me, please.

I thought for a minute. Melly straddled my ankles. She leaned forward, her hands on my knees trying to convince me with her wide-eyed gaze.

OK. I will.

Yay!

We kissed and sealed the deal.

Thank you for helping me, Melly.

Of course. Tonio, when you ask me for help, I'm going to help you.

It's hard for me to ask.

I know. You want to do everything for yourself. The ladies that come into *El Centro* – that's the hardest part for them. Coming in and asking for help. Some folks don't know how to ask. I know you. You don't want to bother people with your mess. But you don't have to be a hero. You can bother me. Anytime. We're hanging out.

Is that all we're doing?

No, no. Much more. You know. We hang out.

Like boyfriend and girlfriend?

I don't like labels. When they ask, I tell people, Yeah, Tonio and me are hanging out. We have fun. But I want you to know I'm not hanging out with anyone else. No one. I want to hang out with you all the time.

Thank you, Melly.

You're welcome, buttercup.

Babe.

Doll.

Bearcat.

Anytime. I mean it.

I know it. Now.

The movie played on flickering in the low light of the

salt rock lamp, half bottle of wine on the coffee table, our feet rocking back and forth, cuddling, contentedly.

I went to the corner store to get a drink, not worrying about the next day because it was Friday and the day would be cool, a breeze, lots of students in other classrooms, PE, plenty of chances to play. It was late and I wanted a beer. Fuck it. I also figured I could move my car so I wouldn't have to bother in the morning.

As I stepped out of the store, someone called out to me. Not by name, but how folks do when they see you around enough and silent nods become what's up, and hey, how you doin. I looked up. It was this tall brother, who I passed a lot on my way to my car, to the gym, to work. He had a handsome *indio* face and a long, thin black braid.

What's up, bro? How you been?

I'm good, man.

Look here, bro, I got these heart supplements, see –

He held out a white paper bag and shook out the goods.

These supplements cost regular $79.99. They're on sale right now at Walgreens for $45. I'll give it to you for $10.

Naw, I'm good, man. My heart is fine.

I got some Levi's coming in, shoes sizes 7 -9.

Maybe next time, bro.

Right on, man. I'll be checking you out, homie. I'll

catch you when I get the new stuff in.

We shook hands and I jogged across Mission and turned onto the dark side of the street, where I left my car. It was in the middle of the block between two overgrown trees.

I walked up to my car slowly. Some young kid was sitting in the passenger seat rifling through the glove box making a new mess of things. The mess was what angered me, made me steam, all the little papers and cards strewn about the interior of the car, all about the floor, and I thought about how this punk was going to make me pick them up one by one, trying to remember what all I had among them, anything valuable, a small important note. Truth was I had long forgotten many of those bits of paper.

I watched him. Then he turned and froze to find me looking back at him. He didn't move right away. Neither did I. We each waited for the other to make the first move. Finally, I stepped back from the car. He watched me carefully. I motioned for him to come out. He opened the door and hung his legs out onto the curb.

Pick up my things and place them back in the glove box. Everything. Where you found it. Don't 'put' them back. Place them back.

He stared at me, kept a watch on my eyes. Then he decided to break. I guessed correct and stepped in his way. I hip-checked him into the parked car in front of mine. He scrambled to get off the trunk. I grabbed a leg and slung him to the sidewalk. As he got to his feet, I grabbed him around the neck from behind, pulled my forearm under his chin. I squeezed hard, tightened my grip as I dragged him down with my weight. He struggled and I wrenched him hard to one side. He moaned. He had a hand clenched on my arm. It weakened and slowly went limp. I was on my knees with his body slumped against me like the *Pietá*, a Madonna with Christ body. I let go and his arms sprawled out. He was a young kid. Familiar. Like anybody I knew in the neighborhood. Like anyone I have ever known.

I rolled him off me. My knees ached. I thought about my window. The passenger door was wide open and I saw all the bits of glass twinkling on the floor. I knelt on the sidewalk breathing heavily. I thought about whether there was anything valuable inside, anything important. There wasn't. Not a thing.

Tommy on the Bus

We stood behind the bigger boys and watched the fight through the spaces between the bodies. Tommy laughed like the older heads and even talked some shit like he knew the dudes fighting, like they could hear Tommy, and they did and they were getting more pissed, and fuck that, they weren't going to give Tommy the satisfaction, who the fuck was he, just a little head maybe a year older than me but taller, gangly, approaching one of them but lacking, hella lacking especially in name, who the fuck was he, just fucking nobody... He got pushed aside and went over the edge. It suddenly got quiet and we could hear the pop before his body hit the pavement. *Holy shit, fucker fell* is all that was said and dudes started getting their shit together and got off the roof and out the park as fast as they could. Tommy's cries echoed into the night sky as us little heads stared down at him holding his leg, trying to figure out how we were going to get Tommy out of the pool.

Damn, bro, remember that shit, how we used to jump off a fucking roof n shit. Some of them fools couldn't even swim n shit. That was maney! Nobody cared though, bro, soon as you hit the water you were going so fast your fucking momentum took you straight to the bottom, and all you had to do was kick and fuckin rocket to the surface n shit then dogpaddle to the side. That was hella fun. Tommy stretched across the bench seat at the back of the bus, knees spread wide open, a big crooked teeth smile…he was a grown-up version of that 12 year old, still long and gangly but a bit filled out but still Tommy from the neighborhood, always a little dirty, white T-shirt a little smudged, blackened fingernails, asking to bum a smoke from me but I don't smoke, *that's cool, taking care of yourself n shit, that's good, I just got out of jail myself, trying to land this job, you feel me, soon as I get off this long ass bus ride.*

And the 14 Mission was a particularly long ass ride, some folks never made it off missing their stops all day long and trying to get home from work, trying to get to work from home, trying to make this appointment for this and for that then make it to a government line for a $3 copy of some document that proves you are who the fuck you say you are and then back on the 14 to make it before that window closes so you don't have to miss any more time from work, any more time from home.

Hey, man, you got a cigarette, but I don't smoke, remember, Tommy, *yeah, that's right, I already asked you n shit. I'm trippin. Ha ha I just need a smoke, man, this is a damn long ass ride. You remember how we used to jump on the back of the J Church and ride it all the way to Day Park, fucking 6 of us n shit holding onto each other. We were crazy, dude. Or riding BART all day long just for the hell of it, kicks n shit, we ain't had nothing better to do so we be like let's ride BART n shit to nowhere. Just jump the gate and be gone all day. Man, I need a fuckin cigarette. This job needs to come through though. PO said he got something for me, so I'm gonna see what's up. Man. I been on this bus forever n shit. Fuckin 3 hour tour n shit. Ha ha. We hella lost on this bitch, you feel me.*

Tommy was a lot like me. *Nicoya* Mission-born, light skindid, about the same age, poor, single mom at home, he had a little sister, I had a little sister, we lived two buildings apart but when I visited his place, I saw how we were different: his apartment was always unkempt, toys and clothes and shit covering the floor, his little sister trying to pick up whenever Tommy's friends were over, no beans or rice on the stove but pots and pans piled high in the sink, *Tommy, go to the store and get your friends some chips or something,* and Tommy grabbed the crinkled bill from his mother's red-tipped hand and was out, me and one or two other dudes standing in the middle of the room, *how are you boys? Still in school?* We were like *it's summertime, señora. Hmm, that must be nice. Playing all day. Running outside. That is nice.* Her voice was raspy and she was young and must have been pretty once, she still had her alabaster skin and her dark eyes were bright, cute freckles on her cheeks but her tussled hair and that dying voice made her a lot older, the door slammed and Tommy rushed in unceremoniously, the large bag thrust out into our faces, I was never comfortable there, as generous as they tried to be, and polite as they were, I felt for Tommy, somehow I felt he might be unhappy. He never let on if he was. He liked being with his friends. Always.

Yeah, man, we were crazy then but the craziest shit was jumping off the roof of the pool. That was sick. It was high n shit right, but you didn't care. You weren't tripping about how high it was or the fact you had to clear the edge, it was like a little step, remember, and if you didn't push off it right, you could trip and spill n shit. But you didn't care, you just wanted to be out in the air, just feel like you were flyin for a split second, free, free as fuck, man, when you was up in the air like that it was like you was as high as the buildings across the street on Linda Alley, it was like you were gonna clear the fuckin roofs and keep going. Free, it was freedom, bro. That's probably why we didn't give a fuck about jumpin off a damn roof. We just wanted to feel free.

Tommy didn't remember things the way I did. I don't think he ever jumped off that roof, I don't remember ever seeing him back

51

up there, just a wave goodbye and *check you guys out* as he split for home whenever we shimmied up the pipes to join the big heads on late nights. Tommy wasn't bad, caught holding a little weed, which ain't about shit except if you're like Tommy and from here and dudes get arrested a lot for a little. Tommy wasn't a bad dude, bro, and it probably wasn't just the weed, it was all kinds of other shit like maybe

You ain't got someone to greet you a good morning
You ain't ever tripped too much about school
Education ain't never did too much to make you trip
You ain't got money
You ain't got good food to eat
You ain't got nice clothes so dudes be clowning you
You ain't got no damn father
You ain't got models except for the fucks clowning you, and
who never leave the park
You ain't ever had someone tell you you could leave
Ain't ever had anyone let you in on the secret
Ain't ever had a thought about where to go
You ain't ever had someone say I love you,
I love you, homeboy,
I love you, Tommy,
No one ain't ever told you you're special, young blood,
God damn it, you're special

Tommy didn't have much now on that bus, no cigarettes, no job, no stop in sight, but he had Tommy, he had himself, he was the only one with the strength and love to rouse him awake every morning, he had himself to keep company as he counted away the seconds tick tick tick, he loved himself enough to take the time to gel his hair and comb it, to clean himself up as much as he could, Tommy was never a very sharp homeboy, but he was still here, still had his chin up just in case a familiar face came through, a friend, he pushed forward, without no other choice because Tommy had a huge heart, he was full of love, had it in reserves, just waiting just waiting just waiting, and Tommy had these stories, he had something to say to whoever was close, just like he did when we were teens and kicking it on the block, flipping cassette tapes on the boom box, he was always jabbering 100 miles a minute about a song, a group, a movie, dinner, a girl, walkmans, the best Chinese food, gold chains, some lost homeboy, *remember him*, Adidas, weed, menthols, the beach, what it's like in San Francisco, the flea market, water slides, weather, the California coast, earthquakes, fuckin Niners. Tommy could talk about it all, hitting a cigarette funny and all the time dancing to the music, a hot-footed high step, back and forth, side to side. He still had his stories. And for four more blocks, me to listen to him.

Next Time

Stopping at the ATM on 16th and Mission, a strung out homegirl reached out to me as I waited in line. I had noticed someone pacing near me, first, behind me and then to my side. But I didn't trip. This is 16th Street. I'm home, right. I know what's up. People trip all up and down this street. People gawk. People stare. People look at you all crazy, and shit. They take up space and are constantly moving. We all just mind our business, right. Suddenly, she tugged on my sleeve forcefully. Not really aggressive but with intention. Confident. She was familiar with me. She wasn't trying to harm me. She just wanted my attention.

Hey. Hey, c'mon.

Excuse me.

C'mon. Let's go.

She wore a grey zip-up hooded sweatshirt. It was open to the chest and I saw that she had a white tank top underneath. Her khaki Dickies were smudged and sagged. Way too big for her and she kept one hand at her waist at all times. Her cropped black hair was pulled back into a bristly ponytail.

C'mon.

She waved at me to follow her.

I didn't move. I stayed in line.

This time she took me by the bicep gently and tried to lead me away.

Let's go.

Where do you want to go?

Her face was as white as mine, alabaster even. She had a few freckles on her cheeks, and many more congregated on her nose. And she had dark, dark eyes. She looked directly into mine, but she couldn't get me. Confused. Caught up. A bit frightened because it was like she knew me but nothing was coming back. She searched and searched, in tiny shifts. Man, she was messed up. Her mouth quaked wanting to talk to me. She just couldn't. All she could muster, with both hands on my arm, was –

Let's go. Let's go.

I can't.

C'mon. C'mon.

I shook my head a slow no.

Please.

And she squeezed me lightly, pleaded with her brow. She tried to get me out of line again, harder this time.

No, I can't.

It was my turn at the ATM.

C'mon. Let's go. I want you to go with me.

I'm sorry but I can't.

She stood next to me as I slid in my debit card and took care of my business. I deposited one check and then made a transfer from one account to another. She leaned into me, shoulder to shoulder. She brushed the hair over my temple with her fingers and watched intently as my hand typed in numbers. Her eyes were all stars.

I touched the 'return card' button and turned to leave.

OK. I have to leave now.

She took my hand. Her face was sticky dirty like she had been eating *coyolitos en miel* with her hands then licked her fingers clean. She was like a little kid.

Hey – what's your name?

Antonio.

Tonio, let's go. Come with me. A little bit.

I can't today. Next time.

Her dark, dark eyes got sorrowful then shone but only for a moment.

As I walked away, she let my hand slip out of hers like we were exes, like it was good once, it was fiery passion and all kinds of fun until we burned each other out but we were always able to talk afterward, right. We could always greet each other. A friendly hug and how are you. *It's good to see you.* Because we were able to remain cool, you know. We stayed friends.

OK, Tonio. Bye.

She had my hand by her fingertips then finally let me go.

She turned around, hiked up her ill-fitting Dickies and headed toward the corner at Mission, winding around and searching, always searching, all scatter minded, stopping to check something in the garbage, in a window, on the ground, jab-step like to avoid someone when no one was in her way, all helter skelter, herky jerky, looking back for me, once, twice, then turning around looking for someone else.

Would It Be So Bad If Something Happened Between Us

The doorbell rings. There is a long pause before it rings again and it continues to ring like that but I'm so asleep I think it's happening in my dreams, right, so I don't get up and who could be ringing my bell all unannounced while I'm asleep, that didn't make any sense so even more reason not to believe the bell is actually ringing, but whoever is calling is persistent, so goddamn it, I get up to answer the door.

Melly's leg is across me and has me pinned down. It takes me a few moments to unwind the covers and work her leg off me. Damn.

I press the buzzer and wait at the peephole. I want to see who the hell it is getting me up so early. I hear the gate open and clang closed. Then three figures in heavy coats and turban-like hats walk into the building and begin to make their way slowly up the stairs. I watch and I wait.

Finally, they make it to my door. Three *señoras*. They stand in triangle formation, each holding up a magazine in her right hand.

I crack open the door.
Buenos días.

Buenos días.

If you have a moment, we have some good news to share.

No gracias.

It will only take two minutes.

No gracias.

Can I ask – have you spoken to one of us before?

No.

What we have is important information about heaven.

No gracias.

I begin to close the door.

It really is important.

I mouth *no gracias.*

The three of them lower their magazines and turn to leave despondent.

Who was it, babe?

Jehovah's Witnesses. Offering me eternal life. I said, no, thank you.

You tell'em.

Melly smiles big and pulls the covers over her shoulder. I let her sleep in and walk to the kitchen.

Tuesdays and Thursdays were my days to wash the dishes when I was a kid. *Abuelita* made everybody wash their own plate after eating and we all filed to the sink to quickly clean and rinse and say a polite *gracias, abuelita* before leaving the kitchen to watch TV, do homework, get on the phone, flip through magazines, sneak out, or plop on the bed looking up at the ceiling, full and content. There was plenty leftover still to wash though – pots and pans and big spoons and large plates. It was no joke feeding so many people.

And it was a trip how quiet the kitchen got in a moment when the last dish was cleaned and the final *gracias, abuelita* given. It was complete silence except for maybe the murmur of the television or the muffled chatter of a private phone conversation somewhere in the long, burrow-like flat. I would be all alone in the middle of the kitchen in the early evening, hating, hating that I had to do the fucking dishes. I gave myself a brief reprieve and allowed myself to stand my ground and refuse to wash the dishes. I let out a voiceless scream in protest. Then I rolled up imaginary sleeves to the elbows and turned the faucet on.

As much as I disliked the chore, I always left the pots and pans as spotless as I possibly could because I wanted my grandmother to be pleased. I fell into a rhythmic scouring, turning the pans inch by inch as I removed the charred crust from the surfaces. My displeasure turned to determination, purpose, a single-mindedness. *Abuelita* would walk in and comment on how clean I got everything, how well I was able to get off all the black. Sometimes she sat at the table and kept me company. She talked to me about playing cards with her friends at the *Centro* and that another trip to Reno was being planned to take a busload of *viejitas* to blow all their saved nickels, or how her feet ached, how her hands ached, how it hurt her wrist when she went like that in circles and that her feet were cold and then she disappeared for a few minutes only to return wearing a pair of my socks, her feet like swollen *nacatamales* and all the elastic thread clearly snapped. *You don't mind, do you*, she'd ask and I'd reply, *no, abuelita, está bien* and then she continued chatting about TV shows like The Price Is Right and how Bob Barker, *ese viejo* she called him, how he charged too much for laundry detergent because it was much cheaper at *Mi Rancho*; she chatted about the lives of starlets from *novelas*, she'd ask me if I knew who so-and-so was, and I'd be like no, and *abuelita* would say, oh, she was the protagonist in the *novela* about the poor girl from the *barrio* who made it all the way to working in an office building, *abuelita, no sé*, she had the boyfriend but then her boss falls in love with her and she doesn't know what to do, *I don't know, abuelita, why would I know*, she was pretty, *bonita, rubia, pelo largo, colocho, bastante nalgas, abuelita, no sé*, and she went on and on until the phone rang and she got up to answer or someone came running in all crazy and she yelled *qué te pasa*, which distracted her long enough to get on another subject. She went through her recipes and told me how to

61

prepare my favorite foods – *lengua en salsa de tomate con petit pois*, lasagna, meatloaf; she talked out loud about her doctor appointments and reminded herself about the prescription she had to fill, she recited upcoming birthdays and calculated how old everybody was turning, how old we were all getting, we used to be babies not too long ago, my cousins must be so-old back in Nicaragua and that would finally get her onto her favorite subject, Nicaragua, the *mercados*, the fruit you can't get here, *nancites, nísperos, mamones, jocotes, pitayas, coyolitos, you can get those here, abuelita*, sí, but frozen and that wasn't the same, she recalled the vendors selling *vigorón* and *quesillos* and *tortas de leche*, her old neighbors, *la Gioconda, la Chela, la Matilde, Doña Gertrudis*, how she missed Nicaragua, it was so much better than here, everything was better than here. Then I'd remind her that a civil war was tearing the country apart, *ah,* she'd say and wave me off.

She couldn't spend the entire time sitting and talking and eventually she got up and started cooking something. She asked me to try what she made to see if it was good, and of course it was going to be good, she was *abuelita*, but she made me try it anyway and I'd tell her it was good, and she'd ask me if I liked it, of course I liked it, so then she would serve me a plate and I had to sit down and eat with her because she took great offense if I ever refused her food. Sometimes, when I wasn't hungry, which didn't matter when she offered food, but sometimes I just couldn't eat anymore so I'd say *no gracias, abuelita, no tengo hambre*, which upset her and then she grumbled *come mierda pues,* which I always thought was a strong ass reply to an 8 year old. So to avoid any trouble and because I loved her deeply, I sat and ate with her even if I felt I was going to fucking burst.

I miss *abuelita*. There are times when I'm home alone and I think about her and I can just cry. Then I think about her telling me to eat shit, and I laugh.

The plates and glasses from last night's dinner are still on the dining table. I look at them for a moment, think, think a little more, then clear them.

I'm washing dishes when Melly walks up behind me and kisses me on the neck.

Hiiiiiiiiiiiiiiiijuepu –

I never heard her.

Did I scare you, Jackson?

Fuck yes, she scared me and I hate, hate, hate to be startled like that. She wraps her arms around my chest, raises on tippy toe to rest her chin on top of my head (she is absolutely statuesque to me, a venus, an amazon) and rubs me to soothe me. When I get angry, I don't shout. Instead, what I do is smother my anger and get quiet. For a long time. And Melly hates it when I go quiet. She kisses me on the neck again and squeezes me.

I'm sorry. I didn't mean it.

I know.

No, honest. I didn't mean to give you a fright. Sorry.

OK.

OK?

Alright.

We kiss proper.

I'm going to take a shower.

Alright.

Are you sure you're OK?

I'll be alright.

I'm sorry, kitten. I mean it.

I know you do.

Melly strokes the back of my head and sidles into the bathroom.

I go back to washing dishes.

Ten minutes later, Melly comes out in her threadbare white robe, stuck to her still-wet body, and her head wrapped in a towel.

There's a big towel in the closet.

No, thank you. I like my robe.

Of all the things you want to keep here, you choose that ratty old robe.

And a set of good kitchen knives. Not that serrated shit

you had.

She adjusts the towel.

What do you want to eat, babe?

I think about it and roll off the contents of the fridge.

We have eggs, bell peppers, sausage, cheese, fruit.

OK…so we'll have soft scrambled eggs with bell peppers, gruyère and mushrooms.

If we have them.

Melly checks the fridge.

Sure we do. OK then. Barrio gourmand it is.

She bear hugs me around the collar and shakes me a bit.

Melly, you're getting me wet.

Oh yeah…

No, not like that. You're getting me all wet. You're still wet and all you wear is that thin ass robe.

She gooses me and caresses my bottom.

Please –

You don't like it when I touch you, lover?

Oh yes, I do. Just not while I do the dishes.

But it's so much fun.

I know it is. *You* have a blast.

It's just that… I can do what I want and you…can't… stop…me.

She strokes my sides lightly with her fingernails.

That's not better.

No?

I know what you're doing.

What am I doing, good-lookin'?

Tickling me.

No, I'm not. *Son caricias*. See, *cariño*.

NO! That's definitely tickling.

I'm being loving, sex kitten.

No, you're just fucking with me because you can.

I try to keep from laughing. Melly squeals with delight. She hugs me again and pulls me away from the sink. I keep my hands high trying not to get the floor too wet. She swings me side to side and droplets fly all over the kitchen. Then she grabs my privates aggressively and growls before she lets me get back to the sink.

I can't help it, dollface. You're just so damn sexy.

Nothing sexy about being fondled while doing the dishes.

You're so much fun to mess with, too.

I know.

Melly bites my earlobe playfully and reaches for the refrigerator. She takes out the eggs, cheese and the rest of what she needs and quickly gets to fixing the soft scrambled eggs. She is suddenly quiet and focused. Melly doesn't talk much when she cooks. She hums though. She stops to play the iPod on the desk then returns to chopping, stirring, sprinkling.

I finish the dishes and set the table. Melly serves us.

Gonna be a nice day today.

Yes, it is.

It would be a shame to spend it inside.

Sure would.

So what do you think, Jackson? Whatever shall we do?

Well, it's still early. Thanks to the sisters who brought the good news. How do you feel about a spirited hike along the 1?

The drive along the coast, the blue ocean, wide open skies, a walk among the tall trees.

Ooh, I like the sound of that. Let's do it.

Right on. I'll clear the table and you can get ready.

I have just the thing to wear.

Melly pops up from the table to go change but stops short and returns to me.

This is going to be a good day.

She gives me a peck.

Thank you for breakfast, Melly.

You are welcome.

We peck again and she spins and bounds on tiptoe down the hallway to change.

It's a fall day in late October and the sky is perfectly clear. It's early and there is none of the midday traffic on Highway

1. Melly has the window down. The air tussles the curls on her forehead as she stares at the waves cresting white in the open water. The Pacific is still blue. We forget sometimes. Sometimes it takes speeding high on a cliff, alone and undisturbed, to remember.

How far are we going?

Gazos Creek.

Past Half Moon Bay?

Yes.

No. Too far.

Moss Beach then.

Perfect.

Melly leans back in her seat and closes her eyes.

That is perfect.

I drive focused on the dividing line because the height makes me nervous and I have to keep from looking into the expanse on some of the turns or I feel like I'll go off the cliff. It is beautiful. But damn.

We pass Moss Beach and I make a left into a parking lot. People like this spot because it's near a secluded section of beach. People are crazy though. They're willing to risk crossing the highway with small children and old people behind them at a point where it is hard to see the cars careening from one direction, I mean flying around the bend, and then they're willing to hike almost straight down the cliff, ass first, just to spend time on a small patch of beach that is way crowded by early afternoon. Not to mention the climb back up and then across the highway again. It is a beautiful piece of beach but fuck that. There is plenty of California coast much easier to get to.

We're going straight up into the hills. Easy access.

Melly opens the hatchback to switch her shoes. She is resplendent in neon peach tights and a pale grey sweatshirt.

If we get lost, at least they'll find our bodies.

As long as you stick with me, kid, they will.

Melly gives me a wink and takes me by the elbow. We start the climb.

Even this late in fall, it's warm enough to hike comfortably in the shade of trees. Man, San Francisco Bay is bad ass like that. Something I never appreciated as a kid growing up in the Mission, but the *barrio* had us too preoccupied to think about the ocean and trees and red-tailed hawks and shit. What the hell were those? But as a grown up, I've learned to do grown up things, and it is nice to have someone to do them with.

The first three quarters of a mile are a steady incline switching back and forth along the cliff. The sun isn't quite over the ridge but the shadows are withdrawing and it's warming up. We're soon covered in sweat. Melly takes long deep strides, her eyes track each step, her breath comes out in brief huffs.

You're awfully quiet.

I'm counting my steps.

Why?

If I don't, I'll fall.

For real?

Yes. I have to go *one-two one-two* or else I'll lose my balance and trip up.

No way. That is funny.

Same thing when I swam in high school. I had to go *stroke-stroke-breathe stroke-stroke-breathe.*

Or else you sank to the bottom like a shark.

I swam out of my lane. Now shut up and let me hike.

We continue the rest of the way in silence. The trail warms up more. It's getting hot, the shadows completely gone. A gorgeous autumn day. At each turn, Melly pushes back her thick springy curls and silently curses herself, *fucking hair.* Finally, we arrive at the top and the trail levels off and we fall into an easy stroll. We stop to look out over the ocean. I hug Melly, pat her ample hips.

How are you?

I'm good. Warm.

You have a pretty glow to your cheeks.

Melly puts her hands to her face. Damn, she is a handsome woman. Arresting. Easy on the eyes. Out of my league, I think to myself.

Oh my god! Look. Look, look!

Melly points and out in the distance I catch a faint spray. It's a gray whale. We watch. After a moment, a second spray comes up, close. It looks like a mother and her calf. We watch for several minutes. More sprays come up here and there.

That's so wonderful. Can you imagine? Animals that big, so close.

Yeah. They're great. It's strange though. For them to be migrating this late in the year. Something isn't right.

Yeah.

Melly's enthusiasm dims for a second but then several sprays shoot up in unison and she perks up again, claps like a happy little kid. The whales pass and we continue along the trail.

How was your week?

Cool. Melly bumps me playfully.

Lot's of the same. Folks come in with a problem. We sit and talk, and hopefully, I can help them out. This one guy walks in though…

Ah ha, tell me the *chisme*. What happened with this joker?

Well, let me tell you.

Melly gives me a wink and a nudge.

This joker wants help like all the rest. He says he has an

issue with a *jefe* at work, and if someone can help him.

I say, of course, *adelante, yo le puedo atender.* And I motion for him to sit down.

He says, I need to talk to a lawyer.

I say, yes, I am a lawyer. I can help you.

Well, this joker stays standing. He looks at me. He looks at the chair. Then he looks around the office. I say to him again, please, have a seat. *Nada.* He remains standing.

Finally, he goes, can I speak to a man?

Now, everyone is out to lunch, mind you. I'm the only lawyer around to help him.

I say to him, there is no one else. They're at lunch, but I am a lawyer. He looks around some more.

Then he says, what about him in the back?

I say, he's the janitor but you're welcome to talk to him if you like.

What did he do?

He walked to the back of the office and spoke to the janitor.

He would rather get legal advice from the janitor than talk to you.

Yes.

Holy shit!

Happens all the time. They come in. I say, *como le puedo ayudar.* They want to talk to a man. And I go like this –

Melly opens her arm like a matador.

Holy shit. Fucking latinos.

Fuck 'em.

We chuckle at the absurdity of it, and then breathe deep because it is real.

Let's pick it up a little bit.

I lead Melly into a light jog. The trail rolls along next to the highway softly rising and dipping and then taking us inland and we run through a grove of trees, cool and shady until we come out near the bottom of the ridge. We can continue inland or return to the highway.

Do you want to go further?

No, babe. This is enough.

We head back along a narrow path next to the highway, cars zipping by, the rush of air kicking up our shirttails and making Melly's curls swarm. It's uncomfortable and we pick it up again. Surprisingly, the parking lot isn't too far ahead.

We're near sprinting when we arrive at the lot and trot to the car. I open the hatchback and Melly plops down.

Whooohooo.

She closes her eyes and breathes in slowly through her nose and out her mouth. I switch out of my damp shirt. Melly changes her shoes. We drop heavily into the car. Melly places her hand on top of mine.

Thank you for showing me this trail. I think I like

hiking.

You are welcome.

This can easily become a thing.

I'd like that.

We kiss. I feel her full mouth press against my lips. Fucking *bocona*, I think. Definitely *guayabuda*.

What now?

Whatever's clever, babe.

She blows me a kiss.

Alright then. Whatever it is.

We pull out of the parking lot and drive.

Melly begins sending me tweets around 12:30 am. She starts with messages asking why I am still taking shifts at the day treatment residence. Because I was still burdened with student loans. I was stupid. I waited too long to act. I was too old to be sagged down with such debt. It was necessity and obligation. *Yeah, but why?* Because Friday night is a mellow shift, those kids that are permitted home visits leave for the night, if not the weekend, which cools out the ones who remain, less energy, less tension in the cottage, they just want to keep to themselves in their rooms. Plus, it lets me spend Saturday with Melly without having to cut our time short. If I had to work a Saturday night shift, which is also an easy gig, it would take away the entire weekend. So, I take Friday night shifts so I can be with her. *But why, babe?* Because I can't make it on teaching alone. Things have moved forward. My pay schedule hasn't. So, I have to struggle. *But why, Tonio?* Because this is all I can do. This is the only way I can make it on my own. *You don't have to, babe.* What do you mean? *You don't have to make it on your own.* This debt is mine and mine alone. *But you can ask for help.* Melly, this debt is mine. Problem is mine. *Babe, you are not alone is what I mean.* Thank you, doll, for real. And then I change the subject.

Since I don't have a smart phone, Melly is left with social media to contact me. Not having a phone is good. The last thing I want in the middle of the night is to wake up these kids because I'm chatting too loudly. The idea is to keep them asleep. Keep them home. Keep them safe. Melly's media of choice is Twitter. She could send me a long ass email, but she prefers to tell me about her night through 114 consecutive tweets. It feels more like a conversation to her.

So, she just got home from a night out with her girls. Vicky, Daisy and Angelica. Oh my god, doll, it was fun. A couple of glasses of giggle juice, Proseco because I don't order anything shitty. Shot the shit with the girls, cut a few rugs. You know, the works. So, we drink a bit, told stories. Vicky about her baby daddy – things are cool, but you know Vicky, right? Yeah, I know, tell me about it. Daisy still living the dream working for the wine importer. We really have to go by the office she says. After office hours – woo hoo! Free wine. Angelica wasn't talking much. She was just like come on, let's dance. So we go out together and take up space, spin each other and dip each other, having a blast. But you know that kind of uninhibited happiness attracts undesirables, dudes try to come into the Sacred Ring because they see us having a good time and think we must want to dance with them because how could we possibly be having fun without them? So, one enters and I spin him away, another enters and Angie spins him away, another comes close and Vicky and Daisy close ranks on him, *nalgas to nalgas*, it's like Bruce Lee surrounded by evil henchmen on an island fortress and we just wa-tah! wa-tah! them away but these goofballs think this is fun, so we decide to get off the floor and go have a smoke. We were at the Cigar Bar so we sit outside by the fountain under the lamps. It's cool and warm and we glisten, and I go inside to buy a cigar. I come back with a cigar. I mean *a cigar*. It looks like something from a carnival. It should be launched into space. A real *cohete*. I light it and we smoke, pass it around and chat and tell more stories and I order a splash more Proseco, every now and again one of us hits the dance floor for *just one song*, but the talk doesn't stop, we're joking now and laughing and laughing, I mean belly-aching stuff, you know fucking Vicky, especially since she's good and oiled up now, co-workers and tricks and her baby daddy and dingalings and her mom and talking straight smack to strange fools, she's too much, so this one guy comes over because he sees us laughing and smiling so that must be an invitation, I must be open for business, open to company because I'm smiling, so he walks over and says it looks like I'm having a good time, no shit, Sherlock, and he asks if he could join me, I say, no thank you, I'm with my friends, but it looks like we're having a great time, he says, he thought maybe he could join us, and I say that was a plausible thought, in reality it could happen, but no thank you, my friends and I were having a date, for real, no, as hard as it was for him to believe, I said, for real. No. He gave a confused nod, he was fucking clueless and left the table, but he stood in a corner of the courtyard and watched us sipping his Midori sour or Appletini or whatever the fuck he was drinking. We have a good time until around midnight and decide to call it quits. We head out and turn the corner and don't you know it, this buster and a buster friend are walking behind us! Hi, he says, like we made an acquaintance, so where's the next party? No next party, I say, just walking to our car. And what a coincidence, he happened to be walking to his car, too, and he started going on about a club nearby on Market and Montgomery if we were interested in another party and continuing the night but by this time Angelica starts a conversation about her mom and we're all listening, we're winding down and

77

not tripping about these two. We get to our car and hop in. This guy continues to drone on about this club if we're at all interested, and he must have been on auto-pilot because he never noticed Vicky and me getting into position to moon him as we pull out and speed away. Daisy said the dude was still talking as we left.

I tweet infinity. A tweet does not do Melly justice.
so can i come get u in am
yeah. fine.
won't u b tired
I'll catch 3 hrs b4 I get off work
r u sure
(thumbs emoji) walk w/ u will energize me
OK ½ *naranja* (emoji) c u
goodnight, gams (H-wood sign, legs emoji)

Melly swings by in the morning and picks me up. I'm tired, who wouldn't be, but she brings me a beet and cranberry and other plants smoothie. Seeing her is enough to pick up my spirits. We kiss good morning, I grab my shoes and we head out. Melly drives and I gaze out the window, sip my drink, watch the mile markers go by until we get to the coast and the water and the crushing white waves. It is clear again today, but the water is restless and a stiff wind whips across the sand shivering the ice plants and dune grass. We go a bit further than last time and pull into a small access road. We decide to walk an empty stretch of beach (there is plenty of it in California) holding hands and chatting pleasantly. The tide is out revealing hundreds of black rocks gathered along the shoreline like forgotten blocks, slick with seaweed and anemones. Melly does most of the talking. She's happy to talk. I'm fine with just listening. It is an entertaining and delightful way to spend the morning.

Later, we arrive at my apartment with all the ingredients for a Mediterranean meal. Melly read that a Mediterranean diet was super healthy and happens to be loaded with foods she loves: roma tomatoes, sun-dried tomatoes, assorted olives, feta cheese, red onion, cucumbers, Brazil nuts, walnuts, cashews, pumpkin seeds, dried figs, grapes, blueberries, herbs and spices, olive oil, a nice goat brille, seeded whole grain bread, and after a bit of digging, a reasonable Agiorgitiko, a Greek red wine. Perfect.

When we get to the top of the stairs, the three *señoras* are standing in front of my door in triangle formation, magazines up. They are perfectly still. Who knows how long they have been standing there.

Buenas tardes.

Buenas tardes.

Melly adds a belated *buenas tardes.*

Ay disculpe la molestia. We thought someone was home.

How can I help you?

Oh, it looks like your busy, groceries and everything, but we'd like to talk to you for a short moment.

As she speaks, I open the door and Melly takes the groceries bags into the kitchen.

Is there something you need?

Ah no, it's about something you may need. *¿Cómo te llamas, jóven? Nunca te pregunté primera vez que hablamos.*

Antonio.

Ahhh…Tonio. Do you mind?

No, *señora*.

Tonio. Tonio. I have a nephew Tonio.

I smile politely.

She smiles kindly back at me.

Señora, someone is waiting for me.

I point over my shoulder to the open door. She peers down the hall to the kitchen. Melly is busy chopping at the counter.

Sí, sí, of course. Just a few minutes. Again, I wanted to present you with a little reading material.

Señora, I've already told you I am not interested.

But this is so important, especially for someone like you.

I don't understand *'someone like me?'*

Un jóven. Right now, you seem happy. You have a companion.

We have a good time together.

Que bueno. But what about when this world comes to an end. What are you going to do about heaven?

Nothing I can do except to be a good person.

But there is something you can do. The answer is here.

All I have to do is read a magazine and I get into heaven. That seems easy enough.

Well, that part is easy but the rest is a bit more work.

The *señora* steps a tiny bit closer. Her backup homegirls follow her, magazines stiff in their hands. She thinks she has me on the hook. She is engaging me. We've been out here for several minutes. I realize I've become a project for these ladies. They know me. They know where I live. They've met Melly. They intend to save me. I look down the hall. Melly is arranging ingredients in a large bowl. She peeks down at me a couple of times.

Señoras, I have to go. I've been rude to my guest.

But we've been having a lovely talk.

You want me to keep my guest waiting longer?

If she understands how important it is what we're discussing, then she'll understand. If she only knew what He can do.

Her backup homegirls chime in unexpectedly loud.

But I haven't told her we'd be speaking so long. I've left her waiting long enough. I have to go now.

I back into the doorway.

Un momento, jovén –

Buenas tardes.

I begin to close the door.

Let me read you a short passage –

Buenas tarrrdes.

I swing the door forward.

At least, take this material.

BUEnas tardes.

I close the door finally.

Man, those old ladies are insistent.

I think they like me. I remind them of their *sobrino*, Tonio.

Is he as cute as you – thick black-framed glasses, crossed eyes and little pug nose?

He must be.

Adorable. Now set the table, babe. I am fucking ravenous.

I do as I am told.

It's timing.

Originally, when we first went out, Melly and I were supposed to go out with another friend, Teresa. We were all at a house party, outside, in the large courtyard of these duplexes where several friends and peers (because they weren't all my friends) lived. The DJ was blasting the music so loud we had to shout to hear each other outside. I was standing by my lonesome drinking Tecate, the 12-pack of beer set between my feet when Teresa walked up to me, *heeeey*, what's up, we greeted each other with kisses, *faire le bissou* as the French say, and she asked me if she could have a beer. Of course, Teresa could have a dang beer, we were good friends, we met as undergrads at Cal and now we were pursuing higher degrees at SF State. I cracked open a beer for her and we toasted *salud*, and then she went, this is my friend, Melly, and I was struck by how much I liked the name Melly. There wasn't much light outside and that only made her dark eyes darker and her winsome smile kinder. She was bundled up in a scarf and puffy jacket, it was San Francisco and she was used to a warmer climate; I was in my traditional short sleeves, always the homeboy. Teresa asked if her friend could have a beer. Of course, Melly could have a ding dang beer. I cracked another one open and the three of us toasted *salud*. We settled into a groove drinking beers and listening to the exaggerated beats, rocking and swaying, toasting fresh beers and feeling an easy buzz. Soon we got to talking about music and concerts and how fucking Prince had played the DNA lounge, holy shit, that must have been live to see him at such a small intimate club, and we named off our favorite songs, "Dirty Mind", "When You Were Mine", "Soft and Wet", "7",

"Alphabet St.", "U Got the Look", man, he wrote so many bad ass songs and that got us onto to writing, poetry and stories and La Raza Writers Workshop and their journal, *Cipactli*, and fundraisers and organizing against Prop 187 and fucking Pete Wilson, man, **fuck Pete Wilson**, yeah, fuck that prick, and we pounded more beers, education, bilingual education, social services, Medi-Cal, funding, who's legal, and then Melly talked about her trip to Cuba, and we were like, that's what we fuckin need, revolution, for real, another toast, tipsy hugs, some *bissous* because we were such good friends, young, creative, motivated, agents of change, man, Bob Marley and Mumia Abu Jamal and Rigoberta Menchú and Che and Dolores Huerta and then Teresa asked if we had seen the Muhammad Ali movie *When We Were Kings* and none of us had so we were like we should all go tomorrow, fuck yeah, hell yeah, and we cracked open more beers and toasted because we had a plan. We were good and buzzing. Then we decided we wanted to dance, so we killed our beers and went on to have one of many great nights.

The next day, I went to meet Teresa and Melly at the agreed upon corner. Only a couple of minutes passed before I caught Melly walking up the street. She was alone.

Hey, Tonio.

Hey, Melly.

We *faired le bissou*. Like the dang French.

Teresa says she's not gonna be able to make it. But we can still go to the movies if you like.

Yeah. Yeah, let's go.

So we headed to the movies together. All the shows for *Kings* were sold out, but we still wanted to watch a movie. We bought tickets for Austin Powers even though we had no idea what it was about, and that show was full too. The only seats we found were at the end of the rows, one behind the other. I took the seat behind Melly. Even though we didn't sit together, we had a blast. When a funny scene happened, Melly turned around to look at me and we shared a laugh. We had a great time. Afterwards, we ended up at Mel's and, over burgers, we made a date to go back the next day to watch the Ali documentary.

I picked Melly up and we caught an afternoon show. It was amazing to watch a young Ali jab in and outside the ring. We walked out of the theatre moved and pumped up, ready to do things. But first, we were hungry. It was evening. We were in Japantown so we went to a ramen house for a nice dinner.

Later, we sat in my car in front of Melly's house and talked for hours like 7th graders. Finally, the conversation died away and it was silent. We sat there looking out the windshield quietly. Then I took a chance. I leaned over and kissed Melly. She kissed me back.

I don't know if Teresa was in on it and the plan was always for me and Melly to go to the movies alone, but we went out for eight months there after – got dolled up for dinner, had brunch, met each other's families, went to BBQs, attended a wedding – until one day Melly told me 'this' wasn't what she had planned for herself, I wasn't included in her plan, I was completely unexpected and too heavy and so much passion and a reason to stay planted but this just wasn't the time, this wasn't going to work, this could not work, and a month later she was gone, I mean *gone*, out of the country. She would blow through town on occasion over the next few lifetimes. She always reached out, made it a point to share a meal, have a laugh, sit for a while but Melly never stayed for too long.

It's all timing.

The California Coast is constantly changing. Imperceptible tremors deep beneath the Earth's crust disrupting the surface continually, around the clock while we sleep and when we are wide awake. Bit by bit the coast crumbles into the ocean unnoticed. Now and then there is a story about an apartment complex suddenly teetering on the edge of a cliff, or a whole house disappears into the water in the middle of the night. One moment there, the next gone. One day all of this will be swept into the surf. Like in a billion years.

Melly feels like eating, but not a complete entrée, she wants to pick on sides, a small salad and, ooh, she wants oysters on the half shell, fresh, fresh, fresh. It's a bad time to drive the 1 because all the other adventurous yet sensible people have the exact same idea, it's going to be a crawl all the way to Half Moon Bay, but Melly doesn't care. It will be beautiful, and if we play our cards right, we can catch a sunset.

One hour and a half later, Melly and I are slurping down oysters and sampling from small plates at the bar of this touristy beach restaurant. The bar area is raised above the dining area. We have a view of the bay and can see people walking out onto the breakwater. The window is enormous. It's like the entire wall is a living painting of the coast. Stunning.

We finish the small plates, slug down the last two oysters and shoot the breeze as we glance out at the glimmering water. The sun is over the ocean and the light floods into the restaurant, reflects off every single polished surface in the room.

Melly is easy to like and she makes fast friends with the wait staff and the bartender, a tiny dude that appears to be standing on an apple crate behind the bar. She moves seamlessly from sipping her drink to talking to me to breaking mid-sentence to ask the waiter for tortillas and that gets the bartender going that someone is tossing them on a comal in the back and the staff within ear shot erupts with laughter and then a young food runner offers to run to the market, for real, if Melly wanted tortillas. Of course, it wasn't necessary but thank you though, and Melly sipped her drink and fed me a cherry. The bartender asks if we're tourists. We say we're from San Francisco but we love to enjoy the coast. *Sí, sí,* he says, it's very beautiful. So you're Americans, he concludes. Yes, we answer together. But you speak Spanish very well, he adds. I explain that my parents are *Nicoya* and Melly is half *Nica*-half *Salvadoreña.* The good half is *Nica*, I say. Melly feeds me a pickled onion. Then the bartender calls out that one of the servers is also half-and-half – half *pendejo* and half *baboso*, and that gets them all howling and going on about each others shortcomings and sexual preferences. Melly and I laugh as they cut each other up. The bartender offers a shot of tequila. Melly says she prefers whiskey but who are we to be rude. We say salud and drink. It's into the dinner hour and the talk shifts from insults to quit standing around and tend to the customers, *guëy.* The energy winds down. The bar is cleared of our plates. The wait staff split up and get to work. There is a calm. I sip on a Bloody Mary. Melly guzzles club soda.

Hold on. I'm gonna get a re-fill.

Melly walks around a corner to the middle of the bar

and leans over to catch the bartender's ear. I look out at the view. A small sailboat pulls into the marina, sails ruffling as it slows to dock. Melly is back with her full glass of soda.

Babe, do you want more oysters?

Hmm…I'd like to order more but it's getting pricey.

Go ahead and order them. They're on him.

Who?

Old gentleman in the bad Hawaiian shirt. Order another Bloody Mary, too.

How'd you work that out?

He's been watching me since we sat down. When I walked over to ask for more club soda, he started chatting me up. He offered to take care of the bill.

Just like that?

Yup.

Why?

Trying to impress me.

He thinks he can get somewhere with you.

Yup.

Even when it's obvious you're with me.

Uh huh. You know, I'm going to order the bruschetta, shrimp in the iron skillet, the arugula salad, and – oh, I don't know – some top shelf Scotch neat.

Alright then. Won't he be impressed.

He sure will.

Melly put in the order and then gave the gentleman a big sarcastic wink and a smile. She is such a ham.

The dinner hour is in full swing. The clamor of conversations and pots and pans from the kitchen fill the room. The servers bring our dishes and our drinks are poured. We nibble and talk as people weave behind us. The sun is setting. The sky glows reddish.

Does it bother you that guy paid the bill?

Hmm…seems odd to me. Aggressive. Like I'm not here. Foolish on his part.

Don't take it personal, babe.

Hard not to. I'll try though.

So, it would bother you if someone hit on me?

Depends. If it was in front of me maybe.

Would it bother you if a woman hit on me?

Melly smiles devilishly.

There is little I enjoy more than time spent talking with Melly. It's so easy between us. And sometimes, unexpected.

I went out with a girl once.

No kidding.

It was intense. Passion. Fiery, you know. It's kind of a mind fuck.

Hmm.

I mean, there was good, but it was all so heavy. All the time.

Melly furrows her brow. It isn't too often that I see her perplexed, disrupted.

Does it bother you that I was with a woman? What would you do if I said I was interested in a woman?

Well, I could say, 'What's she got that I don't got?' But then … you know… the hoo hoo.

Melly smiles her girlish smile. Happy.

All I have are two arms, a pair of sensible shoes and my timid way of telling you how much I love you.

Oh – you love me?

Yes, I do.

Like 'in love' love me?

Yes, I am like in love.

You should say it more often. It looks good on you. Brings out your eyes.

I'll try.

There is no try. Only do or do not.

I smile my childish smile. Happy, too.

That's a bit modern for our banter.

Expand the mind.

Simplify, man.

Turn on.

Tune in.

But stay a while, cupcake.

We raise our glasses.

Well, thinking about your sex bunny, I imagine she's easy on the eyes. Tall. Red lipstick. But she's different than you. Much. She can't be just like you. That would be like pushing two negative charges together. Who could stand that? Besides, there is no body like you, tomatuh. My two bits.

Actually, she was frumpy.

Frumpy?

Yeah, kind of Friar Tuckish. Burlap sack and coarse clothing.

Always got to be the pretty one, don't you, doll?

You know it, dreamboat.

Bearcat.

Peach.

My girl.

Not sidecar or anything like that. Just a few laughs. Some kicks.

Like in love.

Like that, handsome.

We kiss. We kiss.

I gotta run and powder my nose.

Melly tweeks my nose and works her way through the crowd to the restroom.

I sit up straight at the bar. I swirl the ice in my Bloody Mary. A basketball game is playing on TVs above the bar.

That is a very pretty lady sitting with you.

I'm a bit startled. The old gentleman in the bad Hawaiian shirt is sitting in Melly's seat.

She is pretty.

A knock out, I'd say. Is she your wife?

No, she's not.

Oh. Then do you mind if I ask her out?

What?

I'd like to take the young lady out.

For real?

Oh, yes.

Hmm…not sure if she'd be interested.

Well, let her decide for herself. You may be surprised.

Hey, man, I don't like where this is going. You're sitting in my lady's seat.

He stands up.

I'll wait for her if you don't mind.

He pats my shoulder. I get furious at his touching me.

Take it easy. No hard feelings.

In that moment, as he's looking at me, Melly comes from his side and hits the old gentleman in the head with an empty beer bottle. It pings loudly and he grabs his head, winces hard. He moves towards Melly but a server intercepts him. He's yelling something irate as the server holds him up. I grab our things and we head out.

What did you do?

He was hurting you. I saw you so upset. I thought the bottle would break and knock him out.

Like in the movies?

Yeah.

Melly bursts out in laughter.

We run outside. I head to the parking lot, but Melly leads me to the beach instead and we run out across the sand. I let her lead me down to the water. We slow up.

Come here.

Melly fishes in her bag and pulls out a small pocket knife.

Come here.

She reaches behind my ear and cuts off a soft curl. She tugs to cut quickly. Then she slashes one of her curls.

OK. Let's go.

Melly pulls me into the bluish surf, the moon bright and three quarters full. We wade in up to our knees. Holding tight onto my hand, she flings our curls into the crashing waves. She raises her hands high, I raise mine, too, and she yells gleefully. Our arms fall into an embrace.

There.

I'm still wearing shoes.

That's a silly thing to do. Why didn't you kick them off like me?

I'm not wearing sandals.

Well, none of this is really important now, is it?

No. No, it is not.

Waves rumble along the shore washing up algae, driftwood and assorted bits of debris. In three days, the moon will be full and the entire beach will be lit, moonbeams shimmering on the water and the bubbling surf rolling up the sand will be visible for a mile in each direction.

The next morning, we stay in. It's overcast and chilly, so we gather all the thick blankets and pillows and pile them on the floor of the living room. We heat up chocolate croissants and make a black herbal tea with wildflower honey, then lay down, cuddle up to watch old movies. The tea is piping hot the way Melly likes it. We turn the TV on to 'Shadow of the Thin Man.'

You know, there is a tiny little street named after the dude who wrote those books?

Whose that?

Dashiell Hammett.

Oh.

We sip carefully and set our mugs aside. Melly stretches an arm across my chest and reminds me that we are a *thing*.

What were we before?

Before, we hung out.

I always thought it was more serious.

It was. For a time.

But not a thing.

No.

Melly fishes out a lipstick from some mysterious keep and dolls up with no mirror.

What if I don't want to be a thing?

Oh, you want to be.

What if I want to be *solo cholo*?

No. You don't want to be *solo cholo*. You want to be with me. Way with me.

Melly plants a big firm kiss on my forehead.

Branded. With me.

I raise up and find an angle in the flat screen. Big rouge lips right in the center of my head.

You remind me of my homeboy, Ariel.

He got tits like these?

No, but one time he tells me how he got together with his lady. He's been married now 19 years. So we were hangin out and I asked him how he met his wife. Now, I've known Ariel since high school and I've known his lady longer than him. She was from the neighborhood. She lived right across the street from a classmate of mine on Folsom and 20th. We were friends, right. So, Ariel and his lady were off and on for a lot early on, for most of the time, actually, before they finally got married. I even went out with her once – to the movies. So, I say, how did you two meet? He says, Well, we were at a house party, and my homeboy comes up to me and says, Hey man, Concha is dancing with some dude. I was dancing with some other girl at the time, he says, so I left her and I split to see what was up with Concha. I walk into the other room and I tap this brother on his shoulder, and I'm like, Hey man, that's my girl. And she's like, No, I'm not. And he says, Yes, you are. And then that was it. They hooked up for the rest of their lives and had like a thousand babies.

So sweet.

That's a *barrio* love story. Two kids get together, they argue, he says I love you, she calls him stupid and then they hook up and have like a thousand babies. The end.

We laugh. Melly rises onto her elbow to sip her tea.

Mmmmm. This is good.

Staying in on cool mornings is good.

We toast our mugs. I feed Melly a bite of the croissant. The doorbell rings.

You expecting someone?

Nope. Not at all. Be right back.

We *faire le bissou*. I go to answer the door.

I check the peep hole. Someone else in the building has already buzzed the gate. The three *doñas* are at the top of the steps reaching into their handbags for their literature.

At first, I turn to leave the door unanswered and just ignore them, but then I stop and give it a second thought. Fuck this, I say to myself and move to answer the door. But before I do, I remove all of my clothes. All of my clothes.

I swing the door wide open.

Buenos días, I say with my hand on my hip.

Initially, it takes a minute for the lady at the front of the triangle to notice. She has her magazine out with both hands and goes straight into her message of salvation and eternal life and the paradise that can be had if I only allow Him into my heart. Then she shifts the magazine to one hand so she can swipe under the title like Vanna White and get to the bullet points, and that's when she sees me, all of me, the way God had intended. The magazine uncovers my paradise to her stunned eyes. Something catches in her throat and stops her speech.

No, please continue. Today I am ready. Today I want to hear your important message.

She walks her gaze down from my face to my privates and is now gawking, flabbergasted. She takes a subtle step back.

Her homegirls must not have noticed right away either because they don't do or say anything. They are busy nodding and backing up their front girl with *sí señors* but when she stops talking, that is when they look up and call out a righteous *Ay, dios mio!*

Cómo está, señora? Hace mucho tiempo.

Joven...su ropa?

I want to hear your message.

But – your clothes.

I didn't want to wait. Your message is more important than clothes.

But, *señor* –

Please. Tell me the good news.

Pero señor, así no puedo.

Of course, you can. *El señor* can do all things. He will give you strength.

In that instant, Melly walks up behind me. She puts an assuring hand on my waist.

Babe, it's cold.

You're telling me.

She slips a warm cup of tea into my hand and walks away. The *doña* peers over my shoulder and sees that Melly is naked, too. She slinks away and her wide bottom disappears into the darkness of the hallway like a large shark into the ocean deep. She is one sexy beast.

Ah, que rico. OK, I'm listening.

By this time, the backup homegirls are already around the bannister and descending the stairs. The front homegirl suddenly finds herself alone. She tucks the magazine under her arm, picks up her briefcase and follows the others downstairs.

I sip my tea loudly, it's still hot, and watch until the three *doñas* are out of the building and into the bright sunny street.

Suspicious Man

The building is quiet early in the morning without the kids around, and most of the other teachers haven't arrived yet. It's just me and the custodian and the principal. A few other regulars will arrive around 7:30. I like to work with the lights out, set the chairs up in the shadows, write on the white board in the dark, pretend like I'm not really there. People will find you if they believe you are in. I want to read my notes quietly. I want to read my emails in peace. This is my time. A space for me before I give it all away.

I write the morning's first objective in the middle of the whiteboard:

Los escritores toman en cuenta sus lectores.

My colleagues praise my printing and ask me where I learned such beautiful writing. Years of practice and modeling for my students, I say. Practice with the kids.

The room brightens. Light floods in from three tall windows that run from the old fashioned radiator almost to the ceiling. Suddenly, I hear shouting. Then distinct pops. Loud reports. A moment of silence. Softer talking. I counted seven pops. The rhythm rang in my head. Three beats then two, one, one.

I check the windows. I can't see much through the dusty screens. I hear talking clearly. I go outside.

A large driveway that leads into the schoolyard is right outside my classroom. At 7:30, the gate is opened. Kids, who get to school early, drop their skateboards and scooters into a large green bin, where James, school security, watches over them, where he's been greeting students and families for decades. When the bell rings, James rolls the bin up the driveway and into his room, keeps them safe until the school day is done.

The yard is empty. The green bin is set in the open gate. Behind the bin is James. I can only see his legs that stick out across the sidewalk. Two police officers stand at each end of him. One is on the radio. The other stands with a hand on his holster. I move closer.

I need you to stay away.

I know this man.

Please, sir…

I said I know him. He works at our school.

The officer meets me. He holds his hand out. I step in so that he touches me.

Sir, you need to move away.

I see more of James. One arm is draped over his stomach; the other is high over his head. I can't quite make out his face.

I'm not leaving. I'm staying with him.

I'm horrified but I keep it together. I call my principal. I stand there, the police officer's fingertips lightly on my shoulder. He tells me it is better if I stand away. I don't respond. I mad-dog him, stare him in the eye. I am not going anywhere.

The police received a phone call about a suspicious man standing outside the school. They arrived at the gate and found James standing there. They questioned him and he did not respond. When they continued, he became agitated and turned his back on them. They directed him to reply. James then began to search around inside the bin. They directed him to show his hands. He did not respond and continued to rummage around the bin. He was mumbling imperceptibly, and appeared further agitated. He was given a final direction to step away from the bin. He came up suddenly with something in his hand. And he was fired upon.

You shot him seven times.

Sir...

You fired at him seven goddamn times.

The principal is with me. He intervenes.

What is this about?

We received a call about a suspicious man standing outside the school.

Many men walk this street at this time of day. Did you question anyone else? Why James?

He fit the description.

Describe who you were looking for.

Sir, we cannot discuss that right now.

You shot and killed James. So he was who you were looking for.

We had a report of a suspicious black man outside the school.

He's been standing outside this school welcoming students for more than 24 years. You could have sent the SRO. He knew James. He would have known there wasn't any problem. Why would anyone make such a call? Even these people, who just moved in across the street...they would have known. If they just looked out their windows, they would see James at this gate every day. These goofy people been here a month, and already they're worried about who's on their street.

Sir, you don't who know made the call.

I know why. They saw a black man outside a school. And you came ready for him.

Sir, we came to investigate a call.

You guys are fucked.

Hey, you're at a school.

A mother with two small children watch us just a few

feet away. Two cars are lined up in the street, blinkers on.

I know where we are. And you guys are fucked.

The principal places a hand on my shoulder then gently turns me away. He engages the police officers. I look at James. He's covered by a white sheet. It's too small to cover him completely. A large spot seeps through around his abdomen. His dress shoes are clean and polished.

More families gather as the four of us stand and wait quietly. The talking is over. There is nothing left to say. More families gather. They are shocked. In the distance, a siren can be heard.

Burn This Motherfucker To The Ground

The wind was relentless, it was punishing, it brought dust and grit and soot and hard rain and icy cold, man, but the folks loved it up there, caught Ubers and Lyfts there, teemed on the sidewalk smartphones and clutches and discreet weed cigarettes in hand as they waited to stream up to the place like ants, man, completely undeterred by the gales and disruptive gusts, they fuckin loved to be under that white tarp and weak-ass heat lamps, not even trippin about the incontinent, ill-behaved typical San Francisco afternoon air, *not trippin*, blood, acting like it was perfectly still, sunshiny, spectacular, them helped along by born-again Manhattans and plenty of them. They just wanted to be outside because *it's sick. It's up on the roof n shit* as one homeboy put it. From the roof they could see the freeway covering 13th Street (which hella folks, who just don't know, claim is not there but they don't understand the power of superstition), the browning stand of cedar trees that line Highway 80 on the way to the bridge, the white steam that rises from washing the bloody, soiled linen in the laundry building of General Hospital. The view really wasn't about shit.

Domingo fell in love with stories when he was in first grade. He got to listen to a story every day without fail no matter how his day went – didn't do his homework, talked too much, was always talking too much, teased but was just playin, took hella long to use the bathroom, said *whoa shit* twice during a reading of some prophet from the old testament who was being convinced cruelly that the Lord was for real, *straight up* – none of it mattered cuz the last half hour of the day he got to sit on the rug with everybody else and listen. Sister Carol was kind, she smiled sweetly, never raised her voice even when he cussed, *Domingo, do not take the Lord's name in vain*, she had tight brown curly hair that popped out from under her black habit, and a long pointed nose. She looked and sounded something like Big Bird from Sesame Street, tall on her stool, cool in sky blue, a book held out above our round heads as we listened intently, followed along as she flipped the pages, pointed to the drawings, had us repeat phrases. It was lyrical, I felt the words move up and down in my ears, I could see the pictures in my mind. Sister Carol was a great storyteller. One time, at the end of a reading, this kid Julio refused to leave the rug. He sat crossed legged, indian style and refused to budge. *Julio, it's time to go home* but he just shook his head slowly, a foolish grin on his mug. *Julio, it's time* and still just a slow shake of his lemon head. Finally, Sister Carol helped him to his feet. A large round stain was on the rug where he sat. The seat of his khaki pants was dark and glistening. Julio decided to piss his pants rather than miss the story. Sister Carol was that good.

The plates clattered above the din of the restaurant, a cacophony of chatter and laughter and shouts, Domingo moved quickly to empty his bin and bus the next table, folks were lined up downstairs waiting for the next open table, and even when there were free tables, people were made to wait, to scheme, to figure out a way to get in, send a text, *I'll call when I get there, or tell'em _____ is up here waiting for you* (cuz I think I'm a baller like that,) or *I'll just come downstairs and fuckin get you, dude,* Domingo hustled to clear tables cuz that was his job, a second job, but work nonetheless and he knew only one way to do it: as best he could. Wait staff slid between the tall tables with orders and he stopped and stuttered, jab stepped, moved in and out with his head down, watched from the periphery for an opportunity to dip into the fray. He stacked the plates and glasses like a game of Tetrus, fit everything up to spilling. *Mingo, can you get this last table, thank you.* It was just a single pint glass and he reached for it like a frog snatching flies but he was too quick, didn't get enough of his fingers around it and tipped it to the floor. It shattered with a *pow* and the commotion waned. An instance of silence.

Damn it, fuck me. He said it under his breath and moved quickly to pick up the pieces.

Then the crowd began to applaud, whistle and cheer sarcastically. Domingo kept his head down and cleaned rapidly but as the noise rose, he stopped his hands working, slowly raised his eyes. He caught site of a table of three white dudes in dress shirts and khakis, he saw them clapping and nodding, enthusiastically, possessed, way too fuckin happy, and bro, my man Domingo took it the wrong way *fuck that* and became incensed. Now he knew and saw and recognized that not everyone in the place was white, there were several folks of color enjoying drinks and the knock off tapas and chatting hella over-loudly while they thumb-scrolled tiny screens, there was even a tall table of casually yet fashionably dressed latinos just to his left, a few feet away having a good time, briefly suspending their conversation and high spirits to watch the spectacle of him; even though these brown folks were delighting in the innocent slip of another brother, there was something about those three goofy fucks that set him off. *Ahh fuck naw.*

Domingo didn't realize it for a long long time, but he liked learning. He liked the feeling of knowing – a word, a definition, a history, dangling participles, King's English, the speed at which objects accelerated, laws of physics, rule of law, the three branches of government, an historic date, a formula, square roots, the first six values of p, Neon, Argon, Krypton, Xenon, Radon, photosynthesis, osmosis, metamorphosis, the line between two points, democracy, plutocracy, revolution, 1776, 1789, 1831, 1866, 1940, freedom only comes through persistent revolt, through persistent agitation, 100 °C or 212 °F, haiku, 17 syllables, couplet, sonnet, prosody, repetition of a sound, Magna Carta 1215, Manifest Destiny, a trail of tears, expansion, exposition, exclamation, my mark, a small pink blossom in the rock, a force, a push or a pull, a Newton, $F = ma$, rest, pressure, oppression, the age of enlightenment, reason, *lumières*, 1972, original sin, free will, a funny little thing like flabbergast, *pantuflas*, self. Domingo came to understand each piece added to the self he was going to be. He owned these small bits of himself, *this is mine* was meaningful to a kid who kept all his personal belongings in a single drawer. It took him some time though, he struggled to read and he hated it at first, but the sisters and lay teachers always made him feel he was bright, it was their love, they always told him he had a wonderful mind, that's why they got so disappointed when he wasn't trying.

But he did try, he tried his hardest, especially for Mrs. Collan, his fifth grade teacher. She was originally from Manhattan, Irish stock, tall and blond and perfectly round breasts, Mrs. Collan was no nonsense, upright in turtlenecks, always corrected Domingo's grammar even when he visited while in high school, strict, disciplinarian, accountable, she had impeccable posture as she moved from the blackboard to the map to the flag and from desk to desk, checking his work, correcting his mistakes, her woman-ness heavy on his shoulder as she leaned over him. She challenged Domingo, worked his ass like no one had before (the sisters just didn't have the clout, sway Mrs. Collan commanded), and she was fair. She was conscious of who he was – latino, poor, single mother –and what were his challenges – *barrio* apathy, crime, other latino boys. She tried to get him, she looked out, tried to empathize.

–How did you feel about that test?

–Fine, Mrs. Collan.

–Did you feel it was more challenging because your first language was Spanish?

–I don't think so.

–Those tests weren't made for someone like you. They were made for students in Iowa with a completely different life experience. So unfair. Ridiculous.

–But I still think I did good.

–You did *well*.

–That's right, Mrs. Collan. I did well.

She believed in him and made no excuses.

Naw, fuck that, these three goofy ass suckers laughing at him just wasn't going to play. To Domingo, in his eyes, this was some straight white people shit. Where he comes from, if you're gonna laugh at people's mistakes, laugh when someone falls and bloodies himself, when someone gets slapped because she didn't speak up fast enough, laugh when someone spills a bag of groceries or loses money that can't be made up, if you're gonna laugh at people when they are down, then you better cop to the fact that you're a plain asshole and be ready to back that shit up because in his eyes, folks worked too hard, opportunity was capricious, happiness was volatile, and their normal was other people's crazy, so they, like Domingo, were a bit overly sensitive about life, he was a bit overly sensitive because he tried goddamn hard each day, *each* day. He wanted to do well because he still believed people like Sister Carol and Mrs. Collan that believed in him since he was a know-nothing boy, *inquieto* and mischievous but curious, inventive and silly with ideas. They liked him and taught him and even loved him enough to keep telling him, filling him with confidence, with the immortal creedo *just keep working hard, Domnigo, keep doing the right things and you will see, you will see…*

It was a moment of peace in the afterschool program, after the snacks were thoroughly pawed before eaten, when homework was done or lost or hidden or outright refused, the balls stopped rolling, the rings on the structure were still, the markers were capped and the glue wiped off the table, pencils were sharpened, paints sealed and collected, brushes soaked in the sink, and the chatter, laughter, cries, whines, and my-turns finally silenced, Domingo put away the last of the goldfish crackers and made a note they needed more.

–Mingo, you coming to shoot pool? Joseph and Ben and them are headed to Hollywood Billiards.

–Naw, I can't. I got a bit of reading to do. I mean, I could but I need to get this reading done.

–What are you studying?

–Archaeology.

–Why are you studying that?

–I want to go on digs. I want to know the story of people and places.

–But why? What are you going to do with that?

–There's a lot to know and still find out. I want to know about where I'm from.

–But there isn't anything here. There's nothing left to find.

Domingo stuck the note to the bulletin board then turned to speak directly.

–A new building, offices right, is going up on Washington near Kearny. They just started excavating the foundation. You know what they found there? Mastodon tusks and bones. In San Francisco, a damn Mastodon. But the developers don't care. They don't want to let scientists come in and document. It would set their schedule back. You believe that? They don't care about finding a Mastodon in fuckin SF.

–That's because it isn't worth anything to them. If you want to make it here, you got to write code, or come up with a sick new game.

–I can't make it as anything else?

–Not here, man.

–I can't choose what I want to be.

–Not here. Not if you want to make money.

Domingo washed out the paint from the last few containers and contemplated his fate.

Domingo set his rag on the floor and walked determined to the table of three white dudes.

–Is there something funny?

–You dropped a glass.

–I know. So?

–You dropped a glass, so now people are applauding. That's what people do.

–Naw. That's not what all people do.

The dude snorted and turned to his friends and left Domingo standing there. They continued to have their fun, and then Domingo thought about making codes and designing video games and it rose up in him like a wave–

–You think that's funny. Is this funny, motherfuckers?

Pow!

He picked up one of his stacked plates and flung it to the floor.

–Is this funny?

Pow!

He flung plate after plate and then glasses at their stocking-less, well-heeled feet as the frustration welled up inside him, the night classes, the summer classes, the student loans, [he was proud of his modest scholarship], the two jobs, the time studying, the applications, the desire, the uncertainty, the insecurity, the creedo and the fallacy. He was lucky his family had been in San Francisco for so long, so he still had a home for the time being, but he felt the anxiety of his neighbors, of the small businesses that disappeared, he couldn't see his place among the new buildings rising downtown. Domingo remembered when he was a kid walking in the shadow of Market Street with his head up to look at the tops of those buildings, he thought the skyscrapers were beautiful, impressive, he daydreamed about working on a top floor. But not these new buildings, these buildings offered nothing for him or his neighbors. *You got to write code*, is what he thought. *You got to write code.* It filled him up.

—You want me to break shit, I'll break every last plate in this fucking joint! Then I'll burn this motherfucker to the godDAMN ground!

He threw more glasses and now he was shouting at them.

—What you see from here is bullshit. What about striving and personal manifest destiny and standing up for what you want to do?

Pow!

A waitress tried to step near Domingo to get his attention. He ignored her.

—Can't we have archaeologists, astronomers, biologists? Can't we have engineers, can't we have physicists, can't we have architects?

The waitress set a hand on his shoulder but he shrugged her off.

—Can't we have historians, can't we have anthropologists, can't we have chemists?

Another waiter stood at his other side but didn't make a move to start him. The glasses came faster and harder.

—Can't we have playwrights, and writers, and poets, can't we have counselors, can't we have social workers, can't we have sociologists, can't we have activists, can't we have community organizers, can't we have people who are interested in people?

They ducked instinctively at the crash, unexpected,

raised their feet, a few women grabbing at their legs to protect their bare ankles from the shards. He saw the surprise then fear in their eyes and it encouraged him.

Domingo then began to turn over plates of food from the tables. A manager came and called his name, tried to talk to him on a personal level, not angry but trying to understand his reason for being angry and calm him down. My man Domingo had none of it and continued his rampage.

—You ain't laughin? I thought this shit was funny. I'm gonna break plates until your hands are bloody from applause, you goofy fucks!

Finally, a waiter and a cook took him as gently as they could and moved him out of the dining area and got him in the elevator and took him down and outside to the sidewalk. Once outside, the cool air struck Domingo and snapped him out of it. He was tense but quiet, still, hands bent like claws and shaking. He stared across the street. He said nothing. The waiter talked to him. Told him everything would be fine. Just take it easy. The cook shook his head slowly.

—Damn, dude, you broke all kinds of shit. Those white folks were scared.

Good. That's good they were scared.

Orlando

Rolando was an overactive kid, excitable, but to his father, my brother Marcel, he was hyper, always running around picking up stuff for a minute and then running to some other part of the house, and my brother could tell where Rolando was at all times because he could hear him, screaming bloody murder because of some shit with his brother Ernesto and then laughing like the devil as he got away after getting his brother back, Rolando was always raising up a storm, temperamental, never sat still, and when he was still, like to draw, he knelt so he had to raise up when he said something, anything, it didn't matter who was there to hear, he just made some comment like 'red sucks, if you only got a red crayon, that sucks – you got to have more colors', and if no one was around, Rolando would just start screaming for his father until he came. *PAP'! Papaaaaaaaa!* Rolando was wild, untamed, never a moment's rest, man, according to my brother, he was fuckin mental as we used to say as kids in the neighborhood. He played too much, messed around too much, teased his big brother and older cousins too much, he jibber jabbered to no end, man. He was volatile, mercurial but in a good way. Rolando was lively – *full of it!* – didn't do anything half-ass, he threw himself into whatever mess, fun he could get into with unbridled enthusiasm, sometimes reckless, once in a while dangerous, *that fuckin kid*, Marcel would say rolling his eyes and shaking his head, *holy shit* … unable to muster up anything else except for *that fuckin kid* and then a chuckle not being able to help himself because at the heart of it all, the little dude was exceptionally funny, had a wit beyond his years, and my brother often told me that Rolando reminded him, that many family members said Rolando reminded them of me. Marcel would raise his brow and wag a finger at me and say *just like you*, man. *Especially that temper.* Loquacious, constantly ruminating, always coming up with shit, easily triggered and got mad to tears. But sassy and charming, a fucking whippersnapper as the English used to say in some fucking long ass time ago. He was precocious and I often told Rolando I knew he was gunning for his *Tío* Tonio.

You ain't me, young blood.

I know I'm not you. I'm me, he'd snap.

But I see you trying to be like me. Think you funny. Think you hip. But you ain't slick, *sobrino*.

Yeah, so what's up then, what?

And he would step to me like he knew anything about *barrio* culture (little soft ass suburbanite *nica*) but all up against me, his little bony chest puffed out (he was built just like Marcel, who I saw in Rolando), fists out to his sides and chin up in the air like a Hollywood *cholo*.

Then I'd smother him in a bear hug and jab him playfully in the ribs whispering, *you ain't so bad, you ain't so bad.*

Every couple of months, I called my brother to tell him I wanted to pick up the boys and take them out.

What's up, Marcel blood.

Hey Tonio. Man, you always call so late.

I'm sorry, bro. I forget if Oakley is three hours ahead or three hours behind.

What the fuck – it's the same time as SF, he'd say cracking up.

I know, man. Oakley is in the fuckin cuts.

I wanted my nephews to know where their father and me grew up, especially since I was still hanging on in the Mission, barely, but I was there and I wanted them to know all about it.

I'll be by early Saturday. Like 8 AM.

OK, I'll let them know.

If I leave later tonight, I should make it in time.

It's Thursday!

Yeah, I know. I'm cutting it close.

Fuckin dude, he'd say cracking up.

I left San Francisco hella early, grabbed a coffee for the ride (and, man, I never drank coffee) and made the trip relatively easy missing all the traffic. I pulled into the driveway and honked. Someone pulled aside the curtain in the picture window but nobody came out. I sat for a few minutes and then unbuckled my belt and went to the door.

What's up, dude? C'mon in.

What the hell? I'm ready to go.

Yeah, I know, these guys are running a little late.

My nephew, Ernesto, came out of the hallway into the kitchen and greeted me.

Hey, *Tío* Tonio.

He hugged me firmly.

Hey, young blood. How are you?

Good.

You ready?

Yeah. Almost.

HEY *TÍO*!

Rolando jumped out at us and slid across the linoleum floor in tighty whiteys and black socks. Then he disappeared back into the darkness of the hallway.

What the –

Yeah, I know, man. Tell me about it. It's everyday with him.

Marcel and I smiled at the thought of the little dude as we waited for the boys to be ready. Ernesto came out shortly and waited with us.

That's it, Rolando. I'm leaving you, young blood.

I walked out with Ernesto trailing me. I let him into the car.

Wait, wait! I'm ready, *Tío*. Let's go.

Tonio, you got to be real careful with him.

We'll be OK.

I mean it. He's a handful. He just takes off.

We'll be fine. Rolando, are you going to take off on me?

No.

What are you gonna do?

Stay with *Tío* Tonio.

What happens if you don't?

I'll get lost.

And how will you feel?

Sad.

You wanna be sad?

No.

Right on. We're gonna stay together. We'll be good, Marcel.

Alright. Take care.

Let's go, young blood.

He squeezed into the backseat, buckled himself in and we took off, Rolando waving furiously to his father through the back window.

There was still no traffic on the highway. Lucky.

Where're we going, *Tío*?

Rolando leaned forward between the front seats as much as he could.

San Francisco.

Cool. What are we going to do?

Everything.

COOL!

I want you guys to see where your father and I, and your *Tío* Johan and *Tía* Dora Luz grew up.

Yeah. Cool.

He sat back satisfied with my plan and watched the landscape travel past the window.

We drove into the City and jetted along Fell Street.

Where are we at?

Fell Street.

Oh.

Ernesto looked coolly out the windshield, leaning back comfortably in the front seat.

This is the Panhandle. Jimi Hendrix gave a free concert there one time.

Who's Jimi Hendrix?

A badass musician from the 60s.

Oh. Cool.

Ernesto said nothing. He scanned the neighborhood and nodded to the radio.

What's this now?

Golden Gate Park. I'm gonna take you to one of my favorite places in San Francisco. The Academy of Sciences. I love this place and now it's all new. It's great.

I parked on JFK and we walked through the square between the De Young Museum and the Academy. Rolando ran ahead to look into the fountains. I called out as soon as he started dipping his hand into the water.

That's nasty ass water.

What? It's water.

All these pigeons poop in there.

Oh, that's nasty.

I'm telling you. We'll wash our hands as soon as we get inside the aquarium.

The aquarium!

Yes.

Do they got sharks?

Oh, hell yes. And rays and a giant octopus and fish that glow in the dark. A white alligator. I think they still have a two-headed snake.

Snakes!

A giant green anaconda, too.

Rolando took off again, this time with Ernesto chasing behind him. He caught Rolando at the top of the steps and grabbed him by the scruff of his shirt. Rolando shrugged off his hand. The two of them waited for me. I took Rolando's hand and we walked inside together, safe.

After washing hands, we walked to the top of the globe that housed the tropical rainforest.

The idea was that this would be an aquarium but they couldn't figure it out. The globe wouldn't be able to hold the water without cracking, so they turned it into a terrarium of a tropical rain forest.

Rolando and Ernesto's heads turned to watch the soft flight of butterflies, mouths open in awe at the size of some. I pointed out the birds and the cacao trees and told them that cacao was found in Nicaragua, too. It grew wild like coffee and yucca up in the *cerros*. From the top, we looked down to the flooded floor of the rain forest and watched the large, fat-sided fish slide in between the giant root structures of the trees, floating, suspended, gills and fins beating easily in the clear water.

We moved from exhibit to exhibit stopping just long enough to catch a glimpse of the animals – southern swamp and the alligator snapping turtles and albino alligator, the Philippine coral reef with dozens of vibrant, pastel fish and undulating, multi-appendaged invertebrates, the creatures of the Amazon including the giant arapaima and green anaconda, and finally the California kelp forest. We found some space among other visitors and Rolando and Ernesto squeezed together against the glass looking up at the swaying kelp and the fish that dashed between the leaves or hid in the rocks.

See that bright orange one? That's called a Garibaldi. It's the state fish of California.

The Garibaldi climbed to the kelp floating on the surface then suddenly dipped back down settling somewhere in the middle of the mass of fish, nibbling on seaweed attached to the rock then hurrying to the tangle of kelp leaves, its orange side flashing through slits in the brown and green leaves.

A leopard shark sailed along the glass right past the boys' wide eyes.

Shark! A shark!

That's a leopard shark. The bay is full of them. They don't get much bigger than that. They're harmless.

We spent a couple of hours walking past all the fish, translucent shrimp, pulsing jellies, stopped to stroke some sea stars –

You mean 'starfish', *Tío*.

No, I mean sea stars. They're not fish at all.

We zoomed through the insect and reptile exhibits, strolled through the African Hall, gawked at the Tyrannosaurus and grey whale skeletons, laughed our heads off in the earthquake exhibit, and missed out on the planetarium shows. We stood outside the immense silver orb planetarium staring down at the rays that circled and soared through the water of a small lagoon.

Rays are cousins to sharks. They're related.

Tío, how do you know so much about stuff?

When my brothers and I were kids, we loved things like sharks and dinosaurs. Whales, tigers. We had lots of books with pictures and we spent hours looking through them and drawing. We loved to draw them, the more teeth the better. I read all those books. I read, man. That's how I know stuff. I read, and I still do.

Ours eyes followed the rays for a few more hushed moments. The din in the aquarium had died down. Most visitors had already left. It was getting late but there was still sunlight outside.

What do you guys want to do?

I don't know.

Are you guys hungry?

Kinda.

Yeah, a little.

Let's do this. I'll show you guys where we grew up, and then we'll find some place to eat. OK?

OK, *Tío*.

I raced the boys across the square, around the fountains and back to the car. We jumped in gassed and giggling from the run. I checked the boys for seatbelts and we turned around on JFK and got quickly onto Oak and headed for the Mission. It was a beautiful day and the streets were crawling as usual. I circled a couple of blocks until I was going in the correct direction on Valencia to point out my old apartment building.

We lived in there on the third floor. The one in the middle.

You lived way up there?

Yeah. For 15 years.

UP THERE?

Yes. All of us.

Rolando and Ernesto pressed their faces against the glass trying to get a good look as we passed under the apartment and by the building altogether.

It's late. Let's eat and then I'll take you two knuckleheads home.

We gonna eat around here?

Naw, not here.

Why not? You grew up here.

Yeah, but I don't want to go anywhere here. It sucks now. People who want to be seen, living like they're on reality TV. Naw, we'll go somewhere else. Drive a bit so you can see more of the City.

Cool.

We went for spaghetti and meatballs and then walked

along the Embarcadero as the lights were coming on and they could see the lighthouse of Alcatraz, the lights along the cables of the Bay Bridge and Oakland and the East Bay. We strolled eating gelato and when they were done, they both ran along the rail jumping and pointing to the darkening bay, they ran and jumped on and off the cement benches, arms in victory V, racing and looking back to check me. I called out when they were too far ahead and they turned around and ran to me, past me then swung around and ran ahead of me again. I called out and then called less and less, let them run, let them scream, let them be them.

Freshman year of high school, Rolando was good enough to make the varsity baseball team, but he chose to play for the JV instead. He would have been playing with Ernesto, which was real cool for Marcel, the thought of his two sons turning double plays, elegant double plays, flipping the ball behind a back and the other hanging in tough then pirouetting to complete the throw to first, it made him real proud, but Rolando did and didn't like the idea, he was just a freshman and Ernesto a junior, so it was pressure to achieve like the older boys, and Rolando knew he could play, compete with them, but he wanted some space, he wanted Ernesto to have his space and not have to trip about his little brother. It was his first year of high school and he hadn't come into his own, *his own,* yet. Things were changing.

The JV played at noon. Marcel and I sat at the top of the bleachers, sneaking sips of Tecate from a freebie cooler bag he got at a Giants game. It was blazing, man, and we were unprotected, but the beer stayed cool. When the boys made a play, we clapped politely and took celebratory swigs from foamy cans. Marcel had warned me too keep cool and not call too much attention to Rolando on the field. I could cheer his name, just not like *Tío* Tonio did at a house party.

I can do that. I can cheer normal.

The boys played clean baseball and it was compelling drama into the late innings when our boys took a one run lead and held on to win. Rolando high-fived his teammates then got in line to shake hands with the other team. I couldn't help myself. I let out one blaring cheer. The game was over anyway.

Get 'em, Rolandito, get 'em, young blood, I called out raising my beer.

Marcel and I packed up the empties and made our way carefully down to the field as Rolando finished chatting with his friends.

Hijo, you played a good game.

Thanks, pap'.

Good stuff, Rolando.

Thanks, *Tío.*

We shook hands homeboy style then I pulled him in for a hug.

That was great fun to watch, young blood. You boys can play.

Thanks, *Tío*.

And there's still more baseball to watch. What time does Ernesto play?

Varsity plays at 5, answered Marcel.

Man, we got hella time to kill.

Yeah, and we can't stay in this damn heat.

Oh hell no. Well, are you guys hungry? We can eat, stop for some beers right quick, and be back for the game. Rolando, what is there to eat around here?

There's a taco place a block away from the park.

Hmm…what else is there?

They got burritos nearby.

Holy shit, is that all there is around here?

This isn't metropolitan San Francisco, *Tío*.

What? What you say about my mama?

No, I'm just saying we don't have much choice like you do in San Francisco, *Tío*. We're in the cuts, remember? We still have to dial up for internet service.

I heard that! Check out this young blood with jokes.

I faked a right to Rolando's ribcage. He covered up ready to laugh.

Marcel suggested a pizza place.

I know it's not North Beach, Tonio, but it's good pizza.

Fine. Let's just get out of this heat before *Tío* Tonio becomes *Tío Camarón*.

We all laughed and headed out of the park.

We took our time working on a thin crust pie. A couple of teammates walked in with their families. Rolando introduced his father and me, and we exchanged a few pleasantries and congratulations then returned to our meal. I paid the bill without Marcel knowing and we headed back to the field for Ernesto's game.

We settled back into the top bleachers.

Tío, do you think we can go to San Francisco next Saturday?

Hell yes. What do you guys want to do?

Well, I'm asking for me. I have an assignment.

Maybe Ernesto wants to hang out anyway.

No, Ernesto doesn't like hanging out with us old folks anymore. His friends have cars and they go out when and where they want.

When and where they want?

Within reason. I have to approve. Next week he's going to a concert.

Who's he going to see – Bill Haley and the Comets?

Ha hah ah shit, no, man. He's going to see Drake.

No kidding. What's a Drake?

My brother and I toasted cans and sipped.

So, *Tío*, I have to go to a museum and write an essay about a work of art I liked.

So you have to go all the way to SF for homework?

All we got are taco and burrito places around here, remember, *Tío*.

You don't want to write about tacos?

I fake jabbed Rolando some more.

No, *Tío*. My teacher won't accept any more papers on tacos.

He jabbed me back.

I can take BART and meet you out there.

That would make things easier. It'll be better when the teleporters are finally finished. Fuckin Oakley.

We smiled at each other, my brother and me sipping more cool beers and Rolando listening to us talk, elbows on knees, laughing about the stupid things his father and I used to do as kids, and asking us how we ever kept things from our mother. Those were good times.

I met Rolando at the Montgomery Street Station next to the coffee stand. He was right on time.

So what's the assignment?

I just have to find something that I like. Then go home and write a short paper about it.

Doesn't sound like such a big deal?

It isn't really. Just an elective class, but it gives me a reason to come out and visit.

Right on, *sobrino*. Let's go.

The atrium of the San Francisco Museum of Modern Art was an ode to geometry. The floor was patterned in alternating bars leading to four solid white pillars that supported the roof over the main staircase. The geometric motif continued up three floors bathed in striking white light that flooded down from a circular window in the roof. It was impressive, not for its design, which was a bit simple, just rectangles set like bricks really, but for its scale and breadth and how it made you cross this wide empty space to get anywhere else in the museum. It made you feel small.

This museum used to be in the War Memorial Building across the street from City Hall. Nobody went there. It was empty a lot. Quiet. First time I went there, I sat in front of this big oil painting of nothing but white. It was just white oil paint on a white canvas. I thought, 'What the fuck is this?' Then I read the curator's summary about the artist they were featuring and how it was about layers and textures and the tiny shadows created by the heaps of paint and how the light reflected off the surface and that actually created different colors. I sat back down and looked at the painting again, for a while, thinking about what the curator said. I thought, 'What the fuck is this?'

Rolando chuckled as we climbed the main staircase.

Alright, this floor starts the photography galleries.

We strolled through the spaces admiring photographs of nature and dusty towns, old canneries, gas stations in the middle of nowhere.

How about this?

It's a picture of a vacuum.

Not any vacuum – that's a goddamn Dyson DC02 Vacuum.

We stared at the photograph without speaking.

You're right. This shit belongs in a fucking catalog.

We moved along.

What do you think of this?

It's a photograph of a station wagon.

No. This is a painting of a station wagon.

Rolando stepped closer to inspect the painting.

This was painted?

Yes, it's called hyper realism.

Hyper realism…over realism…how can you go beyond realism? Nothing is more real than reality. This is it, he said holding his arms out palms up.

And maybe that's the idea. The goal is to get as close to reality as you can. It's about fooling the mind. This is all an illusion.

Oh, I don't know. It's a station wagon.

It's what we see every day.

The telephone pole, the dried up vineyard, the cul de sac, Oakley. That's too much reality for me.

So, you flee to San Francisco for some old-fashioned, acid trip, free love, hippy ass, whiteboy coocooness. It does feel good to walk around so many free people. It feels easy. But don't be fooled. That's an illusion, too. Plenty of people are hurting in SF. Not everybody benefits from the 'open-minded' attitudes. Never stop questioning, young blood. Do you like this one then?

Let's see more.

Right on, *sobrino*.

We stopped in front of three paintings by Matisse.

What do you notice?

It's like he's trying to use all the colors on his palette.

Matisse was always trying something new. He was always working out some new technique or idea. He didn't always succeed, but it led to his successes. He was inspired, man. He was a '*fauve*' – wild.

We sat on a bench and studied the paintings quietly. Rolando took out a small notebook from his coat pocket and jotted down a few notes.

I can't believe they have a picture of a vacuum in here.

Do you think it doesn't belong here?

This is one of the largest modern art museums in the country. People come here from around the world. They're going to pay all kinds of money to look at a picture of a vacuum cleaner.

Andy Warhol painted a damn can of soup, and people lost their minds over it. Maybe it wasn't so much about the can but what people said about it. That picture has you trippin. It has you thinking. Maybe that's the piece that you write your essay about.

I don't think I have anything good to say about it.

You don't have to like it.

The teacher said write about something you liked.

Maybe it's more important to be honest. Say what you think about finding a vacuum cleaner in an art museum. It'll be a better essay.

Do you always tell the truth, *Tío*?

When people talk to me, when they ask my opinion, I try to be as honest as I can. Let's say I'm talking to a family about their kid, one of my students, I have to tell the truth, so they know what they're dealing with, so they know how to support their kid. It doesn't help to lie and say yeah, this kid's doing fine, this kid's alright. They know that ain't true. They want to hear that their kid is OK, and he is OK. He just has challenges that he is always going to deal with. This is who this person is. Lying changes nothing.

So, you always tell the truth?

I think it's important to speak your mind, especially when it's something difficult.

Will you always tell me the truth?

I will always shoot you straight, young blood. I will always be honest.

Can I tell you the truth?

I hope you do. I will always be here for you.

Anything I want?

Anything you want.

I think I will write about that stupid vacuum.

Good. But don't just say it's a stupid vacuum.

I'll be smarter than that.

You always are.

We sat in front of the Matisse and talked about colors and the time I spent in France and the Centre Georges Pompidou and French bohemians and Krishnas along the Seine on New Year's and maybe someday the two of us would be walking along the quay if Rolando decides to travel for school like I did but maybe it won't be Paris because he didn't study French, maybe it would be Japan and he'll be teaching English but that would be after graduation, which was still some time away, he had time to think about it, right now he could just focus on what he wanted to do in college, or better yet Rolando could just focus on high school and writing this little forgettable paper on a vacuum cleaner featured in this prestigious institution, he could just think about sitting on a beautifully lacquered oak bench in front of a Matisse in the perfectly conditioned air at the SFMOMA chatting with his *Tío* Tonio, wondering whether or not they should get hot dogs, or maybe find a nice place to sit down and eat well. Naw, never mind, let's get hot dogs and walk around downtown, he said. It was a gorgeous day outside.

Eventually, Rolando played varsity baseball for three years (the first with his brother), and he found his space and the balance between practice and studying and breezed through high school. Like his *Tío,* he dug reading and soon he was equally passionate about books and histories as he was about playing ball, so much so that USF recognized that spark in intellect and decided to award his efforts with an academic scholarship. *What about Berkeley, I said. It's cool but USF seems right, you know, Tío.* So, Rolando graduated honoring us all and was set to go off to college. Marcel had asked him what he wanted as a present, and Rolando was quick to say he wanted to visit Nicaragua. *Are you sure, Marcel asked, it's the rainy season right now in Nicaragua. That's fine,* Rolando answered, he wanted to experience the rain and the worms that rose out of the mud and the unrelenting humidity and the dusty *mercados*, he wanted to see the view of the cobblestone street from the window of Alfonso Cortés and stand in the intersection of *los cuatro caídos* and swim to the shores of *Solentiname* and make rubbings of the petroglyphs on *Ometepe*, he wanted to eat legitimate *bajo* and maybe try *garrobo negro* and walk barefoot over volcanic rock because as he understood it was everywhere. Not to be bound by the landlocked, dry grass landscape of Oakley, Rolando grew up proud as hell to be *Nicoya* just like his father was proud. He read the great poets and looked up history and when the opportunity came, he was ready to make the pilgrimage to Managua, couldn't wait to walk out onto the simmering tarmac, the hot breeze blowing in his face and the palm trees succumbing and bent around him.

Rolando traveled with his grandmother. Marcel reminded her, too, to watch out for him. Mama, you know how he is? he said. *¿Qué le va a pasar? Mamá*, watch him. He's never been down there before. *Todo va estar bien. Verdad, hijo?* And Rolando squeezed his grandmother tight, smashed a kiss into her cheek then took his father's hand and shook it thank you, gave him a warm embrace and told him how much he loved him and not to worry. He wasn't that crazy, manic little boy anymore. Only a little bit. Be safe, *hijo*. I am, pap'. I always am. And then Marcel let his little boy go.

At the airport in Managua, Rolando jumped in the back of a pickup with the luggage and a small boy he did not know. His grandmother rode up front with his *primo* Luis. He held on tightly to the bed of the pickup as it sped along the highway to Granada, he smiled big taking in the passing landscape, the black boulders in basalt fields, the towering silhouettes of *Sandino* atop the *cerros*. Tears dragged from the corners of his eyes but he didn't care; he was happy to be sitting on the luggage in the back of a rickety truck, a small strange boy looking at him curiously, at his shoes, at his hair, at the abalone buttons of his denim shirt. Rolando was happy to be careening along the highway, shelled and ruined from years of civil war, heading home.

When he wasn't occupied eating *vigorrón* from a banana leaf or downing huge cups of *pinolillo* (plates and cups appeared all the time all day and at each new residence), whenever he could, Rolando, little notebook in hand, sat down to talk to his grandmother and her sisters as much as he could to get down their stories, he was intent on documenting, or at the very least remembering what life was like for our family in Nicaragua, what life was like for most *nicoyas* in Nicaragua.

¿Habla español? His *Tía* Daisy looked at him with kind eyes and a pleasant smile as she rolled *masa* on a large wooden table.

No, no tanto. Es que allá es puro inglés con su hermano.
Entonces, no habla español.
Algo.

¿El Marcel no le habla en español?

Sí, algo. Conmigo también trata.

Sí, entiendo, abuelita.

Ya déjalo en paz. His *Tía* Adela set two pieces of *leña* in the old cast iron stove. She stoked the fire, then began to gently lay slices of *plátanos* in hot oil.

Aquí, él va a aprender hablar. ¿Verdad que sí, hijo?

Sí, tía.

Claro que sí. Aquí se va a artar de gallo pinto y cuajada como un buen indio nicaragüense. ¿Verdad que sí, hijo?

Sí, tía.

Tía Daisy motioned for him to stand next to her and she showed him how to cup a mass of *masa* in his hand and pound it out into a perfect tortilla. That was the way she had learned when she was a little girl, standing at the shoulder of her mother, his great-grandmother Berta Wenceslada, that's how she learned to make many things – *chancho frito, arroz a la valenciana, bajo, huevos en catre, cerdo asado, cajeta.*

Your *bisabuela* would stand over this same table and pound out tortillas all morning. I remember the sound *tun-tun tun-tun tun-tun. Una hecha. Tun-tun tun-tun tun-tun.* Another done. The whole time she had a cigarette dangling from her mouth. Just dancing there.

No es cierto. My mother never smoked when she made tortillas.

Yes, she did. I remember her in the kitchen. Always smoking when she cooked.

Mentira, she would have dropped ashes in the tortillas. *Estás loca.*

Tía Daisy and *Tía* Adela went back and forth like that all day all the time, and Rolando listened to the rhythm of their banter, the lilt of their voices as they spoke, and he jotted down the words of note like *chigüines, chunche, chele, púchica*, and *idiay, idiay, idiay.* His *Tía* Daisy snuck glances at her nephew while she continued to make tortillas. She smiled curiously as he scribbled into his little book.

¿Te gusta escribir, Rolando?

Sí, Tía.

¿Qué escribes?

What I hear. How you talk. New words.

Tía Adela stopped cooking to look at Rolando.

Parece mucho al Reinaldo. Los ojos. El pelo.

Looks just like him.

¿Quién?

Un hermano de nosotros. He died young.

Hmm… he looks just like him. Chele. His eyes. His hair.

¿Mi tío?

Sí. He liked to write, too. He wrote little things – a poem, a little story, a few lines. He sat in his chair outside by himself writing. He left his notebooks everywhere. You look so much like him.

Tía Daisy tossed several tortillas on the *comal* and stacked them just as quickly when they were done. *Tía* Adela brought over *plátanos* and *queso frito* and they all sat to eat. His grandmother served *chía*.

After they ate, Adela went into a small dark room and came out with a large black leather album. She sat next to Rolando and turned the pages. She named the faces, pointed out his grandmother as a toddler, the three sisters dressed in *huipiles*, a stoic photo of their mother Berta Wenceslada.

This is your *Tío* Reinaldo.

Oh.

See, your eyes are like his.

Tía, who is this?

That's me.

Tía, you're so beautiful. She was posed looking up into a hidden light, her long dark hair laid across her shoulders and back, silky and shiny.

Tía, did you ever marry?

Hmm...*muchos enamorados*. But never a husband. No one worth the time.

Adela smiled mischievously.

Wow, *Tía*, you're so beautiful in these pictures.

She turned more pages and named more relatives.

It was the afternoon and the heat was reaching its peak.

Rolando, are you tired?

A little, *tía*.

Do you want to rest? You can lay down on that bed.

No, estoy bién.

Yes, rest. Your *abuela* and I are going to run some errands. Rest for a while. Later, Luis wants to take you out, so you better rest.

Sí, hijo, descansa un rato.

OK, *abuelita*.

The bed was in a cool corner of the room. Rolando laid back slowly and let out a long sigh, the tiredness having built up inside him all day. He folded his hands across his chest and closed his eyes. Then suddenly, he got up and reached for his notebook. He scribbled a final note before laying back down and finally, going to sleep.

Luis was *Tía* Daisy's only son. He lived in Managua and worked as a painter. He hand-painted the large billboards found all over the capital. After picking them up from the airport, he had some work to finish but wanted to take Rolando and his grandmother out and show them a good time.

We're going to go out and eat the most typical dishes.

La Miriam's Restaurante Las isletas de Cocibolca was a neighborhood restaurant that had been in business for more than 20 years. Rolando's *nica* family were longtime neighbors of the family that ran the restaurant. Luis went to school with La Miriam, who was the principal proprietor of the business. Everyone ate at La Miriam's.

Te va a gustar. Típico nicaragüense.

Luis entered calling out *cho cho!* and greeted everyone sitting at the many tables in the large dining hall. He shook hands and hugged a man who appeared to be very familiar. A good friend. Rolando followed the three little old women inside.

The friend hugged and kissed his grandmother and *tías* and asked where they all wanted to sit.

Outside, directed Luis.

It was still humid but comfortable outside. A soft breeze blew in from the lake and the mosquitoes had quit their buzzing and dispersed.

What can I get for you, *amor?*

Bring some sodas and ice. And then some *tostones* and *huevos de tortuga.*

Y tú, amor. ¿Qué quieres?

Miriam, this is my grandson, Rolando. He's visiting from the States.

Oh, mucho gusto. Miriam Valladares. What can I bring you, *amor?*

Rolando tripped that La Miriam was really Mario, but

for as long as anyone in the *barrio* could remember, and for as long as it mattered, he was known as La Miriam and it was loving and respectful and everyone knew him and accepted him. Miriam was a great host, generous, charismatic, funny like *nicoyas* are. He had a command of the place and you couldn't help listen to him when he recounted some trivial event, like all the people sitting around them did, because he brought everything to life and made it grander than it could ever dare to be. He made Rolando feel welcome. *Estás en tu casa, amor. You are welcome here as long as you want.*

Abuelita, why does he keep calling me '*amor*'?

That's how they talk when they own a business. When you walk through the *mercado*, everyone calls you amor. *Cómo estas, amor. Vení ver lo que tenemos, amor.* They want you to buy.

The tostones and turtle eggs arrived and bottles of 7UP. Luis ordered whole fried fish for everyone. La Miriam set large plates of *gallo pinto* and *queso frito* and they all served themselves and ate and Luis kept asking for more ice, which began to melt as soon as it was set on the table, and Miriam called for a boy to hurry and keep bringing out more ice because the 7UP was warm and then it became critically urgent once Luis ordered bottles of Flor de Caña, so the boy rushed out with bowls of ice and cut limes. Rolando's grandmother warned him to be careful and she scolded Luis to leave him alone, he was too young, he didn't drink back in the States, but that was the whole point, Luis said, Rolando came to Nicaragua to learn about Nicaragua, to live like *nicoyas*, to realize that he in fact was *Nicoya hasta la polla*, as *indio* as anyone of them, that he had always been one of them, so Luis splashed some rum over ice and squeezed a lime into the glass and toasted to Rolando arriving to the country of his grandparents, toasted to his achievement and wished him to return many many more times. Rolando drank, easy at first, heeding his grandmother's warnings, but soon he and Luis were good and drunk and Luis began telling bawdy jokes and Rolando howled with laughter even though he didn't get any of the jokes and they all laughed with him, laughed at the fact that he didn't understand any of Luis' stories. The sun set and it became dark, the lights of the tourist spots on the lake visible, Rolando did you know there are sharks in the lake, no, no he didn't but he wanted to see them, *vamos pueh*, and Luis got up to go and Rolando happily joined him but his grandmother and her sisters stopped them, grabbed their sleeves and ordered them to sit, Miriam took Luis by the arm and told him to behave, to give his cousin a good example, *que no fuera tan baboso*, how could he think to go down to the lake at that hour, he was drunk and talking crazy, no, stay, *amor*, stay and eat some more and stop drinking and keep his cousin company. Stop embarrassing himself in front of his mother, Daisy. Sit down, *amor*.

Luis sat down and so did Rolando. They ate a bit more, and drank a bit more against the old women's wishes until they both had to be carried to Luis' truck and driven home by a relative of La Miriam. Rolando was dizzy as he rocked and was jolted to and fro on the drive home, the sky was dark and pinpricked by stars he never saw back home. The stars gathered in smudges, twinkled fiercely, shone a light Rolando never knew existed, yet had been reaching him all along.

Rolando settled into his dorm room nicely. He got along well with his roommate. They weren't the best of friends but they chatted pleasantly and respected each other's space and time. They shared some meals and hung out once in a while but if Rolando chose to keep to himself, it was fine and vice versa. It was a good set up.

Rolando went home every other weekend, and of course, his *Tío* Tonio checked up on him. He gave Rolando a Giants cap and T-shirt to help him acclimate to the City.

He wore his cap proudly, like his *Tío* Tonio and father would, all over campus. On his way to the library. At the office of the registrar. Standing in line at the student union building.

Are you a for real Giants fan?
What?

You're wearing a Giants cap. Are you a fan?

Well, yeah. It was a gift, but hell yes, I love the Giants.

You like baseball.

I didn't have a choice. My family is Nicaragüense. You have to love baseball.

No shit. Me, too.

You love baseball, too.

Yeah, and I'm *Nicoya*. It's just that hella folks around here wear caps, but that doesn't mean they're fans. They just like wearing caps.

He scanned the bookstore. At least a dozen students wore caps.

My name is Jairo.

Rolando.

Where you from, Rolando?

Oakley.

Holy shit, that's hella far.

Yeah.

You must stay in the dorms.

I have to. I've never seen you around.

No, I live at home.

What? Here in San Francisco?

Yeah. My parents been living in the Mission for a long time. We still got our flat.

No kidding.

Yeah, lucked out. Landlord is cool. Hey man, you want to go to the game Sunday? I got bleacher tickets.

Those are great seats.

Almost all the seats are good in that stadium. So you want to go?

Yeah, man. I'm down.

Here, let me get your cell. Let's meet in front of the statue of Willie Mays. But in case one of us in running late, we can call.

OK.

Right on, Rolando. I'll check you out Sunday.

What time?

Noon. 12:15. Let's try to catch batting practice.

OK.

I'll check you out.

Later.

Rolando stepped forward in the check out line. He watched Jairo stride away. He was decked out in a cap, Giants starter and black jeans. It was an unusually hot and sunny day.

The buzzer sounded continuously until I hit the button to the gate. I waited in the doorway to see who came up the stairs.

Hey, *Tío*.

Hey, young blood.

Is that Rolando?

Melly pushed between us before we could embrace and hauled Rolando inside. She rushed him into the living room, where she crushed him with a hug.

It's so nice to see you. Sit, sit. The last time I saw you, you were just a little boy. Maybe you don't even remember. OK, so the cioppino is almost ready, but I have some stuffed mushroom caps in the oven. I also have a charcuterie platter of olives, nuts, artichoke hearts and a few slivers of prosciutto and sopressata. I'll put some together on a smaller platter so we can eat here on the coffee table.

Melly bounced into the kitchen and began clinking and clanking things together.

Do you like *mariscos*, Rolando? she called out.

Excuse me.

Do you like seafood?

Yes.

You're going to love this cioppino.

She continued her clinking and clanking.

Does Melly always cook fancy like this?

She loves to *prepare* meals. She says she used to cook for the nuns in the convent, so she learned the art of cuisine. She's a great cook, but I have to say her *maduros* are lacking.

My *maduros* are bad-*ass!* Here, you boys can start on the mushrooms. You're not allergic to anything are you?

No.

Good because everything is delicious.

She went back to prepare the olives, nuts and Italian meats. I offered the plate and motioned for him to take the first mushroom.

Tío, how long have you known Melly?

I met her when you were still a small boy. You must have been two. We took you and your brother to the zoo, you know.

I don't remember. What happened with you?

Hmm... not sure. Maybe we were too young. Met each other at the wrong time. Had different plans.

And now?

Maybe now is the right time. We've always been friends even if lots of time would pass before we saw each other. We'd go out and then go separate ways.

So you're seeing each other again.

Yeah. We're 'hanging out' as she puts it.

Tío, are you and Melly serious?

She's my girlfriend. We're adults in a relationship. I take that seriously.

Do you love her?

I do. Very much.

How do you know?

Even when she isn't here, I'm thinking about her. I can

be occupied at work, in a meeting, and soon as I'm done, Melly is the first thought I have. I like being around her. Always have. It was always hard when I had to let her go, but I had to accept that.

Now you're together again.

Yes.

Are you going to marry her?

What? You trying to start something? We're in a relationship and we're cool. We're 'hanging out.' Ain't that right, bearcat?

You bet, Ambercrombie.

Melly turned around with flare and blew me a big kiss.

But you talk about it, right, *Tío*?

Look, young blood, I love her. We're together.

Is she going to move in?

Hey, let's try to enjoy this food.

I can hear you two.

So maybe you don't get married, but you guys know you want to be together as a couple.

Yes, the door is open for us to spend all the time we want together. I'm happy. And she tells me she's happy.

Tío Tonio.

What's up now, young blood.

I'm gay.

Right now?

Yes, and for a while. I wanted to tell you first.

I looked directly at Rolando. He smirked at me. He looked relaxed. Pleased.

OK. Are you doing OK? I mean – your dad, your mother?

I haven't told them yet, but I will.

Does Ernesto know?

I think he figures something, but he hasn't said anything. He always watched out for me.

Like big brothers do.

I didn't say anything for a moment. Melly came and sat down between us. She put down the platter with assorted olives, artichoke hearts, small pickles and slices of prosciutto and cubes of sopressata.

Are you two still talking about me? I heard you the whole time.

No, babe. We're not talking about you.

I just told *Tío* that I'm gay.

Oh. Come here, baby.

Melly hugged Rolando.

I'm glad for you, Rolando. If you need us, you know you can come to Tonio and me.

I know, Melly. That's why I told *Tío* first.

He's also trying to get me to make you *Tía Melly.*

So what? I kinda like that. I don't know about the

married part, but I can still be *Tía* Melly, Rolando. It makes sense. I'm going to be around here for a while, baby. Right, Jackson?

You said it, Jane.

Melly punched me in the shoulder then slipped an olive into my mouth and gave me a smooch. She encouraged Rolando to try the soppressata, she had bought a spicy kind, delicious, and splurged on hazel and Brazil nuts. Rolando went for the pickles, typical *nica* to prefer the vinegary options, but she told him to make sure and try at least one cube of soppressata, the cioppino was almost ready, we would eat soon but until then we nibbled and I asked Rolando about school and how it was going, had he talked to his brother, I needed to have them both over together soon before the season was over so we could order pizza and watch a game, no, no, no, Melly could make the pizza, a margherita and some regular kind like pepperoni only she would layer it with delectable Italian meats, did Rolando like the soppressata, she could throw that on the pizza and pancetta and ooo culatello, top it all with fresh organic broccoli, holy shit, let's just order a pizza, you be nice, palooka, let me take care of the food that's eaten in this home, are you hungry, Rolando, the cioppino is ready, and we moved to the dining table, half in the kitchen – half in the living room, and Melly served the stew in large bowls, poured a glass of red for the two of us (I didn't let Rolando have any wine) and we ate, chatting about books and writing, if I was working on anything and I was, a little bit at a time afterschool when my students were long gone and it was just me at my desk and the custodian polishing the floors in the hallway, I wrote little passages in the afternoon emptiness of the school building, when it was finally quiet, wasn't it better to write at home, well, home was a little different now that his *Tía* Melly was spending more time with me, less peace as there once was, oh, you love me being around and don't be such an *exagerado*, you have plenty of time alone, you can write all you like but you choose to be with me, I do, cuddle cutie, damn straight, doll, oh I forgot the bread, Rolando, do you want some bread, and before anyone could answer she was up and slicing a small loaf of focaccia, she set a small basket down and served more red and sparkling water, we thanked her and let Melly know how fantastic the cioppino was, she was a marvelous cook and some looker, too, she kissed me several times during the dinner, and squeezed Rolando's arm, it was a wonderful dinner, excellent really, we enjoyed every bit of it, yes, we did, it could not have been any better.

After his lone trip to Nicaragua, Rolando always longed to go back and visit different parts of the country – Managua, for starters, as crazy and potentially dangerous as it was but it was the capital, Estelí, Chinandega, Corinto, Poneloya, El Chocoyero, Chontales, Rama, Bluefileds, Little Corn Island, Rivas, Peñas Blancas – but first, he was going to Florida, *Florida?*, yes! and checkout the *Nicoya* stands in the sunshine state and be surrounded by the culture, but why Florida, well, he grew up in the suburbs and didn't experience what me and his father had experienced, so he craved to be deep in the middle of a large *Nicoya barrio*, the streets saturated with *fritangas* and *bajo* and *chancho frito* and people yelling at each other from one side of the street to the other all the time in the recognizable diction of his grandmother, *idiay*, and he wanted to walk in that interminable heat and have the choice of *refrescos* to drink – *chicha, chía, pinolillo, pitaya, horchata, tamarindo* – plus, it was on the way to Nicaragua, and Walt Disneyworld was there! What? Yes, he wanted to go to the Magic Kingdom, so what, he worked hard during the school year, saved his money, and now he wanted to spend it and have fun, *OK, hijo, have a good time. I will, pap'. I will.*

It was late in the afternoon when Tonio finally sat down and caught some news. He asked Melly if she had heard what happened in Orlando. Yes, she said, she heard about it early in the morning. The radio cut the music to break the story. 49 people dead.

Marcel confirmed that Rolando was in fact at the club, a friend of Rolando's from USF, someone Marcel knew, had reached out and mentioned that Rolando had gone to the club with him and their other traveling companion. He was hurt. Bad. He was taken to the hospital. He was deeply sorry, Mr. Padilla, and began to blubber near the end of the phone call, Marcel held on and waited to hear the end of the message. Rolando had died at the hospital later that morning of multiple gunshot wounds. He held on for a long time. He almost made it to the afternoon.

I saw another report from the continuous television coverage on the TV above the treadmill, but this one was different in particular because the faces of the dead were finally broadcast. It struck me how young the majority of the victims were. How young and beautiful and promising and happy they were. Stanley Almodovar, 23. Oscar Aracena, 26. Omar Capo, 20. Peter O. Gonzalez-Cruz, 22. Juan Ramon Guerrero, 22. My eyes welled up and something leapt out of me when Rolando's face came on a little more than halfway through the slideshow. Rolando Antonio Padilla, 21. It had been almost a week and I had been trying to keep things together like Marcel wanted for us to do, Marcel wanted to find peace quickly, there was a small gathering and brief service because nothing could ever suffice, it would never be right, so the best thing for everyone was to get on, man, let go, he didn't want to hear it anymore, as sudden as everything had occurred, he would spend as much time in grief, fuck everybody, he was done, so everybody should do the same, *alright, blood, if you need me…,* I'm cool, bro, he said, *I know, man, but for whatever reason, blood,* and he said he was cool, *but I need you, too, blood, we are all in pain,* not like me, bro, *OK Marcel, but I'm here, I'm around,* and he waved me off and set me back on my path, got me to my routine and finding ways to distract myself, walking, running and making sure I got to the gym by a certain hour, but it was too soon, it would forever be too soon, and I could not still the hurt, and did not hold back the tears too well as the broadcast rolled. Marcel said Rolando had been struck four times, once through the cheek that fragmented his beautiful boy, ruined his perfect smile, that's why he had decided to have Rolando cremated because he couldn't stand for anyone else to see him in that condition, that was not Rolando, it wasn't who he had become and Marcel wanted to keep that perfect smile intact for everyone else. But then as the faces slid by, and each image had a sincere smile or a shy grin or a selfie sneer, I began to smile myself, bigger the more I thought of that precocious little boy, a joyful fury, aggressive and rough, kind and thoughtful, that little boy that used to gun for me and try to outwit me, that grew into a man taller than me, which wasn't saying much, as Rolando used to say, reminding his *Tío* Tonio that he was a biddy ass dude, *Tío* Pipsqueak, *Tío* Small frye. As I ran, I began to laugh, out loud, as I picked up the pace, feet pounding hard, thinking about that young face, how funny he was, how accomplished he was, how proud Rolando made us all. I would have that with me always. My *prima-hermana*, Marisol, used to say that she was fearful, seriously afraid of the day that our grandmother would die. From the day Marisol was born, our grandmother loved her infinitely. It was an enormous love that would not end after death. Marisol knew that our grandmother would follow her even after she died, and Mari was fearful to turn around one day and see our *Abuela* Mercedes standing there. Man, I hoped it would be like that with Rolando, that I would be walking down the street in the Mission, which was appropriate because the Mission was always a stomping ground for our dear ones, and I would see him. I was enormously thrilled and pleased at the thought of turning one day to find Rolando dashing around a corner, snickering, playful, forever playful.

Norman Antonio Zelaya was born and raised in San Francisco, CA. He has published stories in *ZYZZYVA*, *NY Tyrant*, *14 Hills*, *Cipactli*, *Apogee Journal*, among others, and he was a 2015 Zoetrope: All-Story finalist. He is a founding member of *Los Delicados*, a latino poetry performance ensemble, and has performed extensively throughout the US with them. Zelaya has appeared on stage, in film and in the squared circle as luchador, *Super Pulga*. Currently, he lives and works in San Francisco's Mission District as a special education teacher. *Orlando and other stories* is his first published book.

info@pochinpress.com
facebook.com/pochinopress

Pochino Press is an *Independent*
Publisher in Oakland, CA

More from Pochino Press

Reflections, A Collaboration Between Painting and Literature by James Gayles

Two dozen U.S. and international writers help create a retrospective of Gayles' iconic portraits of historical and cultural figures including Miles Davis, Celia Cruz and Nelson Mandela.

From East Oakland With Love, by Chamuco

The linocuts of East Oakland artist Chamuco Cortez come to us inspired by a legacy of Mexican popular art. These pieces masterfully bring art to the people, to communicate information for resistance, and to convey pride in *la lucha*, pairing selected works with poetry by Oakland writers.

Slide by Monica Zarazua

The entanglement of private and community memory, place, and the body, forbidden locations and unexpected connections are a focus in these seven stories.

Hunting for Izotes by harold terezón

Cleverly mixing humor with social commentary, award-winning Salvadoran American poet harold terezón shares a collection of his favorite poems exploring family, love, and identity. The cultures of El Salvador and the United States are woven throughout his tales yet masterfully written with universal appeal.

---

www.pochinopress.com